MW01075774

COLLATERAL DAMAGE

A TEAM REAPER THRILLER

THE CABAL BOOK 1

BRENT TOWNS

WOLFPACK PUBLISHING
— EST 2013 —

Published in the United States by Wolfpack Publishing, Las Vegas

Wolfpack Publishing
6032 Wheat Penny Avenue
Las Vegas, NV 89122

wolfpackpublishing.com

Paperback ISBN: 978-1-64734-182-4
eBook ISBN: 978-1-64734-042-1

Library of Congress Control Number: 2020939693

COLLATERAL DAMAGE

This one is for Sam and Jacob

"As soon as men decide that all means are permitted to fight an evil, then their good becomes indistinguishable from the evil that they set out to destroy."
Christopher Dawson

"It may be necessary temporarily to accept a lesser evil, but one must never label a necessary evil as good."
Margaret Mead

"Bollocks!"
Raymond "Knocker" Jensen, 22 SAS

Worldwide Drug Initiative

General Mary Thurston: Bravo
Luis Ferrero: Zero

Team Reaper

John "Reaper" Kane: Reaper One
Cara Billings: Reaper Two
Carlos Arenas: Reaper Three
Axel "Axe" Burton: Reaper Four
Richard "Brick" Peters. Reaper Five

Bravo Team

Brooke Reynolds: Bravo One
Pete Traynor: Bravo Two
Pete Teller: Bravo Three
Sam "Slick" Swift: Bravo Four
Doctor Rosanna Morales

CHAPTER 1

Lashkar Gah, Helmand Province,
Afghanistan

The faint smudge of a dust storm blew in off the desert as the convoy of eight vehicles bounced their way along the barren street. On each side were numerous compounds—some still intact, others partially destroyed, the result of many airstrikes over the years of the ongoing War on Terror—acted as a funnel, an almost perfect killing field for the Taliban insurgents who occupied the capital of Helmand Province.

Three Humvees with fifty-caliber machine guns were in the center of the fast-moving column. The others were white SUVs driven by the Afghan National Police. Their destination was a large compound a kilometer from the city's western edge. It had been utilized by British armed forces in the early stages of the war as an outpost, small in comparison to Camp Bastion, some kilometers north of the city.

In October of 2014, Bastion was handed over to the Afghan forces. A month later, once the British and American forces had withdrawn, it became an Afghan base and was renamed Camp Shorabak. Since then, a small contingent of British soldiers had returned in an advisory role.

The smaller compound, which was the destination of the relief convoy, was the base for twenty civilian contractors hailing from numerous countries, who were currently helping to rebuild different parts of Lashkar Gah. They had a personal detail of four armed security experts provided by the mother company, deemed sufficient for the job with the aid of the Afghan National Police.

The police presence, however, vanished during the night like smoke whipped away on a fierce wind, leaving the contractors to discover their vulnerable position when they awoke that morning. The four-person security team seemed vastly inadequate to keep the contractors safe, especially in the wake of intelligence coming over the HESCO wall—the Taliban had begun to infiltrate the city and was preparing to attack the compound.

The call for reinforcements had yielded mixed results, but a small team of six British Commandos from Camp Shorabak had arrived an hour earlier. The commanding officer there, worried about a ruse, released the British advisors to help. Combined, they and the contractors created a force large enough to do little except fight and die valiantly in the face of the reported number of Taliban.

The incoming convoy would swell their numbers by six. Three Humvees conveying American operators were escorted by a force of fifteen Afghan National Police, who were to continue on to Camp Shorabak after seeing the Americans safely to the compound.

The passenger in the front of the leading Humvee was dressed in desert BDUs like the rest of his team. Each wore armor, with their vests weighed down by extra ammunition. Wraparound sunglasses shaded his eyes from the harsh Afghan sun, and his arms cradled a Heckler & Koch 416 carbine.

Reaching up, he pressed the transmit button on his comms. "Bulldog One, this is Reaper One, copy?"

John "Reaper" Kane waited for a reply from the leader of the Commando force within the compound. Known as "Reaper" because of the tattoo on his back, Kane had been an ex-recon Marine in another life before leaving the service to work in the private sector. Fate had intervened some time back, and he found himself in command of a team of badasses, with whom he'd been fighting side by side for what seemed like forever.

His driver, Cara Billings, had once been a Marine lieutenant as well as a deputy sheriff. She was his second in command, as well as being Team Reaper's sniper.

In the following Humvee was Richard "Brick" Peters, a large ex-SEAL with a shaved head, a beard, and tattoos. He was the team's combat medic and was currently manning the fifty-caliber machine gun fixed in the turret.

His driver was Carlos Arenas, a family man and former Mexican Special Forces. He was now part of Team Reaper.

In the third Humvee were Axe and Traynor. Traynor, call sign Bravo Two, was a former DEA undercover agent, and Axe, Reaper Four, was an ex-Marine recon sniper. Both men were unshaven and had been with the team from the beginning.

"Reaper One, this is Bulldog One. Read you Lima Charlie, over."

"Sitrep, Bulldog One. We're two minutes out and would like an open door to drive through."

"Copy, Reaper One. Situation is fluid. At the moment, the approach is clear, but we're getting all sorts of ICOM chatter, so things could change in an instant."

"Roger that, Bulldog. Situation is fluid. Reaper One out."

More drab sandstone-colored buildings whipped by as they careened along the narrow street. Then it was as though a scythe had cut a giant swath through the landscape, wiping out everything in its path. The result was a large, flat open area with craters and destroyed mud-brick walls scattered throughout. At the center was a large compound with HESCO walls and old gun fortifications around its perimeter, leftovers from the British occupation in the early years. Cara followed the vehicles in front as they drove through an opening before slamming on the brakes to prevent caroming into the white SUV directly ahead.

They all climbed out, and Kane saw a tall man in combat gear headed in his direction. "You Reaper?" the man asked.

"That's me."

"Sergeant Richard Todd, Third Commando."

"John Kane. Just call me Reaper." He went on to introduce the rest of his team and then asked, "Where do you need them?"

"An extra gun on the gate would be good, and two more on the west side. You wouldn't have a sniper by any chance?"

Cara stepped forward. "You got me."

"Rooftop on that building there, ma'am," Todd said, pointing at the tallest structure inside the compound. "It'll give you a clear field of fire for three-sixty."

"New call sign, Cara," Kane advised her. "'God-mother.'"

"Roger that."

Cara jogged off to set up on top of the drab gray-sided building. Kane asked, "Where are the contractors?"

"They're sheltering inside the building where your shooter is going. Center of the compound seemed the safest place for them. It was reinforced early on when this place was first occupied."

"What about their security detail?"

Todd chuckled. "They up and ran when things got too hot."

"Fuck me," Kane said with a shake of his head. "I noticed a good field of fire coming in."

"Didn't used to be. I was here in oh-six, and there were a lot of buildings close to the compound then. It was like an outpost in the middle of Indian country, as you Yanks would say. Three months of solid fighting and airstrikes did the rest."

"Any update on what we're facing?"

Todd shrugged. "Any number of Taliban. Ever since ISAF took out the bulk of the troops on the ground and the country was left with mostly advisors, they've been on a hard recruitment drive, and their activity has picked up. Then there's ISIS. ICOM chatter says there might be some of them in the mix."

As the compound was suddenly filled with shouts and the sound of revving engines, Todd growled, "What the fuck?" as he saw the ANP starting to pull out. "Where the fuck are they going?"

"They're going to Shoraback," Kane told him. "They're under orders. You're lucky we were in the neighborhood, or you'd be on your own."

One of Todd's men came jogging across the compound. "Hey, Toddy, chatter just picked up. It looks like the Taliban are hitting Shoraback."

The sergeant looked at Kane. "That explains them leaving here in a hurry. Maybe we'll get lucky."

"Let's hope so," Kane agreed.

"Did you see many Afghanis on your way in?"

Kane shook his head. "Not one."

"Fuck."

"You figure it's a ruse?"

"You served in the Afghan before?" Todd asked.

Kane nodded. "Twice."

"What was the one thing that happened before an attack?"

Kane knew, all right. "They all clear out. The attack on Shoraback is a decoy. We're the target."

Kane pressed the transmit button on his comms. "Zero? Reaper One, copy?"

"Copy, Reaper One."

Zero was Luis Ferrero, the operation's commander. He was a former DEA agent in his late forties with graying hair and a solid build. Team Reaper, now formally known as the Worldwide Drug Initiative, had originally been his baby.

"We're on station, but we're under imminent threat. Do we have a UAV in the air, over?"

"Wait one, Reaper."

"You got air?" Todd asked.

"I hope so."

"So do I."

"Reaper One, I have confirmation of a Gray Eagle onsite," Ferrero said.

The General Atomics MQ-1C Gray Eagle was an upgrade of the MQ-1 Predator and was driven by a heavy fuel engine, which gave it better performance at higher altitudes.

"Copy," Kane replied then, "Bravo One from Reaper One, copy?"

Bravo One was Brooke Reynolds. She was the team's UAV pilot. Like Ferrero and Traynor, she was ex-DEA. She was an athletic woman with long dark hair and was tough like the rest of the operators. "Go ahead, Reaper One."

"Is the Gray Eagle locked and loaded?"

"Roger, Reaper, the bird is armed with two GBU-forty-four/B Viper Strike laser-guided glide bombs and two Hellfire missiles. We've got enough life in the engine for a time on target of twenty hours."

"What about ISR?"

"We're working on that, Reaper One," Teller's voice came over the comms. Pete Teller was the second seat of the UAV flight team. He had come to them courtesy of the United States Airforce. "We'll let you know when we have something."

"Roger, Bravo Three. Be aware that ICOM chatter suggests that in addition to Taliban, we could be looking at ISIS as well. Also, the ANP have pulled out, and there's been an attack on Shoraback."

"Reaper, this is Bravo."

"Go ahead, General."

General Mary Thurston, in her early forties, was an ex-Ranger Rhona Mitra lookalike, and the overall commander of the teams. "We're aware of what's happening at Shoraback. The Taliban are attacking the base."

"Ma'am, ICOM chatter indicates that is a feint and the target is here at Lashkar Gah."

"Copy that, Reaper One. Prepare as best you can. What's the score for the home team?"

"Twelve, General. Plus civilians."

"Ammunition?"

Kane looked at Todd. "What's your ammo like?"

The Brit pulled a face. "We're OK, but—"

"We could use more, ma'am."

"I'll see what I can do," she told him. "At this point in time, all air assets have been deployed to support our allies at Shoraback."

"Copy, General. Reaper One out."

"I guess we're on our own?" Todd asked.

Kane nodded. "You got that right. They'll do their best to get us something, but all air assets have been routed to Shoraback. You got a map of this place?"

Todd reached into his pocket and took out a hand-drawn picture. Kane looked at it and started issuing orders to the rest of his team, pointing in the directions he wanted them to go. "Traynor, on that building there. Axe, set up the M two forty-nine on the front wall near the gate. Carlos and Brick, you take that building there. Get to it."

"I have a question," Axe said to Kane.

Here it comes. "What is it?"

"These Brit guys."

"Yes?"

"Have they learned to speak English yet?"

Kane rolled his eyes, looked at Todd, and shook his head. "Don't ask. It's a long story. Go, Axe."

"I'm gone."

Todd looked at Kane. "If we don't get extra ammo or reinforcements, it's going to be hell on Earth if they hit us in force. We'll be able to hold for a time, but we'll take casualties and no mistake."

Kane knew he was right. "We're used to situations like this. If I had a buck for every time we were up to our necks in shit, I'd be a rich man."

"Tell me something, Kane. Who are you people?"

Kane gave him a wry grin as he came up with the best way to describe his team. "We're like DEA Special Forces on steroids. We go into places we're not allowed to be and drag narco bosses out by their balls."

"Good team of operators?"

Kane nodded. "Cara used to be a sheriff's deputy. Before that, she was a lieutenant in the Marine Corps. Axe, he was Recon like me. Good sniper, and one of the best men to have on your side. Carlos was Mexican Special Forces, and Brick was a SEAL. Now we all go downrange together and fuck up bad guys' days. What about your lot?"

"All good men," the sergeant said. "Every one of us has done more than one tour in all manner of shit shows."

"Let's hope this isn't one of them."

Todd looked at the sky. "It'll be dark soon."

"How are you guys for NVGs?"

"We're good."

Kane looked around the compound and noticed the lights on each corner of the walls. They were pointed in to illuminate the interior. "Can we get those lights spun around so they're facing out?"

Todd nodded. "No problem. However, they won't do much good. None of them work. I've got to see to my men."

Kane made his way up to the sniper nest where Cara had set up with her M110A1 CSASS Semi-Automatic Sniper System. She had a couple of extra magazines laid out beside her, as well as her NVGs ready to attach to her ballistic helmet. Todd had been right—atop the building, she had a full three-hundred-sixty-degree field of fire.

"How's things?" he asked her.

"I'm not sure."

"Oh?"

She looked through her scope once more. "I picked up some movement out there to our east, but it seems to have stopped. I thought I saw a couple of fighting-aged males with weapons, but they flitted between the buildings, and that was it."

Kane raised his HK 416 and looked through his Prismatic scope. He scanned the area but saw nothing. Then he pressed his transmit button and said, "Bravo Three, copy?"

"Read you Lima Charlie, Reaper One," Teller replied.

"Is ISR up yet? If so, is it picking up anything two hundred meters east of the compound, Pete?"

There was a pause before Teller said, "Wait one, Reaper."

While he was incommunicado, Kane continued to use the 416's optics to scan the area. A minute later, Teller came back to him. "Negative, Reaper, we have nothing at this time. Is there a problem?"

"Not sure. Cara thought she saw something."

"Leave it with me. Bravo Three out."

"Reaper out."

"I've got an itch, Reaper," Cara said without averting her gaze.

The team leader nodded. "Yeah, I've got the same one. Keep your head on a swivel."

"Roger that."

———

It was early evening, and the orange fireball in the west was hovering just above the horizon. There was still a good amount of heat in the desert air, but once the sun was gone, the chill would settle in. Kane had been getting regular updates from Bravo, but so far, there was nothing new to report.

He'd gone around the compound and talked to the commandos. All seemed to have their heads on the right way and were switched on like their commander.

"Kane, you got a moment?"

He turned to see Todd coming toward him. "What's up?"

"ICOM chatter just spiked. Something's coming down the pipe."

Kane checked his watch, then pressed his talk button. "Bravo Three, Reaper One."

"Copy, Reaper One."

"Our comrades have just had a spike in ICOM chatter. Is there anything on ISR?"

"We can't see anything, Reaper."

Cara's voice interrupted over the comms. "Reaper, you'd best get your ass up here."

Kane glanced at Todd. "Come on."

They jogged to the building and up the stairs to the dusty roof where Cara was situated, but neither man was breathing hard when they reached her. "What is it?" Kane asked.

"We've got visitors on wheels," she said, not taking her eye away from the scope.

Kane raised his 416 and looked through his scope. Although it wasn't as powerful as the one on the CSASS, he could make out vehicles and a dust cloud beyond the western edge of the city. Beside him, Todd did the same.

"What do you make of it?" Kane asked Cara as he lowered his carbine.

"They look like civilian vehicles. They could be ANP, and ISIS likes to use them as well."

"Keep an eye on them," Kane ordered. He pressed the transmit button on his comms and said, "Zero, we have—"

He paused.

"Eight," Cara told him.

"Confirm eight," Todd agreed.

"We have eight vehicles coming toward the western side of Lashkar Gah. At this point, we're not sure if they're ANP, ANA, or Islamic State, over."

"Copy, Reaper One," Ferrero replied. "Wait one."

Kane frowned but waited for Ferrero to come back. When he did, the news wasn't good. "Reaper, we're getting reports that the Afghanis have bugged out of Shorabak. It seems the Taliban have joined forces with ISIS and are making a sweep of the area. I suggest you get the hell out of there while you still can."

"Do you have numbers, Zero?"

"Best estimate is two or three hundred fighting-aged males."

"Fuck me," Kane hissed. "All right, Luis. I'll see what we can do."

Kane signed off and turned to Todd and Cara, who kept watching the convoy on approach. "The Afghanis have bugged out of Shorabak and left it to the Taliban. Best estimate is two or three hundred fighting-aged males. We've been ordered to get out while we can."

"I'll get my men organized," Todd told Kane. "Although I don't know how the hell we're all meant to get out of here."

Kane turned in a full circle as he searched for a way out of the city that didn't involve walking. Not only did their numbers include them and the Brits, but also the civilian contractors.

"This is a non-fucking event," he cursed. "There's no way we all get out of here without finding transport for us all. And at this point, we're short a damned bus for the contractors. We stay."

Todd's face set hard. "I haven't had a good scrap in a while. Let's do it."

"Cara?"

"Just say the word, Reaper."

"Zero, copy?"

"Copy."

"We're negative on exfil."

"Say again?"

"I said we're staying."

"Shit. Now is not the time to go all fucking gung-ho, Reaper. You need to haul your ass out of there now."

"We don't have enough transport to get us all out of here, and if we get caught in the city on foot, we're screwed. Besides, we don't know who's who in the zoo."

"Damn it, Reaper! Wait one."

Thirty seconds later, Thurston came on the net, demanding, "What's going on, Reaper?"

He told her the same thing he'd just told Ferrero. Once he'd said his piece, her drawn-out silence made him nervous. Then the general came back with, "Keep me updated. I'll see what I can do from this end."

"Roger that, ma'am." Reaper sighed in relief.

Finished with the general, he turned his attention back to the approaching column. By now, it had entered the city and was racing toward them. "Todd, with me."

The two returned to ground level and jogged across to the south wall, where Axe had set up the M249 next to the gate. They climbed up and leaned against the rough surface of the HESCO wall, their weapons at the ready.

The convoy roared out of an adjacent street and headed directly for the compound, kicking up a small cloud of dust as it approached.

"Who the fuck are these guys, Reaper?" Axe asked, tracking their movements with the M249. "You want me to light them up?"

"Just wait a moment, brother," Kane said, not taking his eyes off the vehicles.

"They look like ANP, Reaper," Todd said.

The convoy skidded to a stop in a cloud of orange dust, and an Afghani wearing a uniform clambered out of the front passenger seat of the lead vehicle.

Todd corrected his earlier theory. "They're Afghan Army."

The man, an officer, looked up at them and waved his arms as he shouted at them.

"What the hell is he saying?" Axe growled.

Kane looked at Todd. The Brit said, "He's telling us to get out of here. The Taliban are coming."

"Ask him how far?"

Todd rattled off something Kane couldn't understand. The Afghani responded to Todd and then spoke again. Todd nodded when the man was done and turned to translate the conversation to Kane. "He says they'll be here in an hour. Those that aren't already here."

The words alarmed Kane, even though he suspected that the city was already lousy with Taliban. "Ask him if he'll stay and fight with us."

Once more, the pair threw words back and forth. "He says no."

"Tell him to fuck off, then."

"Fuck off!"

The officer gave Todd a confused look, and Kane smiled. The Afghani waved a dismissive hand and climbed into his vehicle. Within seconds, the convoy was off and running once more.

"I guess we'd better get ready," the Team Reaper commander said.

"We could set up the fifties in the old gun emplacements before we get down in the muck," Todd theorized.

Axe let out a groan. "Good grief."

"What's wrong with him?"

Kane said, "He can't understand English."

"What?"

"I understand it," Axe growled. "I just can't understand the way these Limeys fucking say it."

"Can you get those guns out of the Humvees, Axe?"

"Sure."

"Wait," said Todd. "Let one of my blokes do it. Leave your man here with the LMG."

Kane nodded. "Do it."

Todd hurried off to get his man.

"Reaper, how many of these guys are we facing?"

"Two, three hundred."

Axe looked over the top of his M249 at the buildings to the south. They were bullet-scarred and damaged, just like the rest that surrounded the small outpost. "I suddenly feel like Davy Crockett."

Kane let out a long breath. "Let's hope this place isn't our Alamo."

CHAPTER 2

Kandahar, Afghanistan

The ops center was buzzing as Bravo tried to keep on top of the activity starting to envelop Afghanistan. The country seemed to be afire, with the Taliban and ISIS suddenly launching operations throughout.

Kabul, Uruzgan, and Helmand were just a few of the provinces under attack from insurgent and terrorist forces. Reports were rolling in about multiple casualties, and dust offs were ordered across the board for casualties, whether they be Afghan or their US/UK advisors.

Sam "Slick" Swift rolled his chair back and rubbed his red hair. The computer nerd let out a long breath before calling to General Thurston, "Ma'am, a report just came in about a SEAL team getting hit in the Khost Valley. They have wounded and a medevac on the way."

Thurston shook her head. "It's like a big uprising across the whole damned country."

"Every US air asset in-country is either being dispatched to the Khost Valley or is on the way to Uruzgan, where the Rangers are pinned down with the ANA."

"So, we can get nothing for Reaper and his team?"

"No, ma'am. Not yet."

"What about the Brits and Australians?"

"The Australians have an SAS team in heavy contact and have asked to be extracted, and the Brits? Well, the Brits are with Reaper."

"Fuck," Thurston hissed between her teeth. "What about our Black Hawk?"

"Ma'am?"

"I know, it's back in fucking El Paso. Pity we can't land our damned C-17 out there."

"Yes, ma'am."

Thurston walked over to Ferrero, who stood watching the feed on a large screen in front of the UAV console. "Anything?"

Ferrero shook his head. "The Brits are insisting that ICOM chatter has gone up, but we can't see a thing on ISR."

"Brit intel is usually pretty good."

"I know, and that's what worries me."

Suddenly a spot appeared on the screen, followed by another. All were outside the perimeter of the compound and seemed to be emerging from the houses.

"Whoa!" Teller exclaimed. "What the—"

"Do a sweep," Reynolds ordered her second seat.

The camera panned to reveal more heat signatures. "It's like they've sprung out of the ground," Teller said.

"That's because they have," Reynolds replied. "Reaper Two, copy?"

"Copy, Bravo One," Cara replied.

"Are you picking up movement?"

"Some to the west."

"You'd better take a look around. We're reading multiple heat signatures that have sprung up all around you. They're coming out of tunnels inside the buildings."

"Shit. Gimme a number."

Reynolds looked at the screen and said, "Best guess is fifty and counting. They're hiding under cover and waiting. My guess is, they'll attack within the next five minutes."

"Roger that. Reaper Two out."

Thurston's face was stoic as she watched the screen. More blips appeared, and the number doubled before her eyes. Before she realized it, she'd whispered, "God help them."

Lashkar Gah, Helmand Province,
Afghanistan

"Reaper, get your ass up here now," Cara said into her comms. She climbed to her feet and swept the perimeter, pausing before continuing the circle. The green haze of the night vision scope gave everything a two-dimensional appearance. Since the setting of the sun, darkness had enshrouded Lashkar Gah; the city showed no lights. It seemed as though all power had been cut, then she saw the headlights. They bounced about far in the distance like small orbs dancing on waves in a sea of green.

"Shit," she hissed in a low voice.

Footsteps sounded behind her. "What's up?"

"Reynolds just informed me we have company," she told him. "It seems we've got ourselves surrounded."

"How many?"

"A hundred at last guess."

"Christ," Todd swore. "I'll go tell my men to stand by."

"They've got reinforcements coming in, too."

"Where?" asked Kane.

"Vehicles coming in from the west."

He could see the lights, bigger now as they drew closer. "I'd bet my ass they're technicals."

"I'd say so."

"Zero, this is Reaper One, over."

"Read you Lima Charlie, Reaper One."

"Are we expecting company from the west this

fine evening, over?"

"Negative, Reaper."

Kane's voice was grim. "Copy. Out."

"We're about to get busy, huh?" Cara commented.

"Yeah," Kane agreed. "I'll be back."

He went down the stairs and entered the room where the contractors had taken shelter. A big man stood up from where he was seated and said, "About time someone came to tell us what's going on."

"I'm sorry," Kane said to them all. "We've been a bit busy, but I'm here now to answer any questions you might have. Just make it quick."

"Who are you?"

"Name's John Kane. You?"

"Mush Thomas."

"All right, Thomas, now that's out of the way—"

"Are you getting us out of here?" another man interrupted.

"No," Kane told him, giving a shake of his head to emphasize his point. "We're here for the duration. It seems the Taliban have risen up across Afghanistan, and we're on our own."

"Give us weapons, then," said Thomas. "We'll fight with you."

"If there comes a time I need you to fight, I'll let you know. Until then, our job is to keep you safe. You stay here."

"Damn it, Kane—" Thomas protested.

Kane held up a hand to cut him off. "This isn't a

democracy, Thomas. Out here, my word is law, and if it ain't me, then you listen to Todd. We're going to get hit real soon by a large number of insurgents and Taliban. The last thing I need to be worrying about is you lot. You stay here and don't move. Got it?"

They all nodded and mumbled incoherently. Kane reached down and drew his M17 from its holster on his thigh. He held it up. "Any of you know how to use this?"

"Most of us can use one," Thomas replied.

The Team Reaper commander passed it to him, followed by a couple of fresh magazines. "Use it only if you have to. If I catch you outside on the HESCO wall trying to be a hero with it, I'm not going to be happy."

With that, Kane turned and walked out. He went across to where Brick and Arenas were perched atop the building closest to the west wall. "You men catch the movement out there?"

Arenas said, "We saw it. What's going on?"

Kane told them. "Make sure you've got your unit one pack handy, Brick. We might need it."

The unit one pack was a backpack full of essential medical supplies for the combat medic to utilize should one of them go down under fire. It held IV fluid, tubes, IV catheters, right down to Band-Aids and safety pins.

"It's right here," Brick replied, patting the pack beside him.

"Good. Keep your heads down."

"Roger that."

"Reaper One, copy?"

"Go ahead, Bravo One."

"Reaper, heads up. Your friends are moving into the open to the south. Looks like they're going to try for the gate."

"Copy. Reaper One out," Kane acknowledged, then, "Cara, Axe, we've got guests to the south."

"Reaper, the technicals have arrived, too," Cara told him.

"On my way to the wall. Axe, if they get too close, light them up."

"Roger that."

As he ran across the compound to the wall, Todd joined him. "Your men ready?"

"As they'll ever be," he said as he fell in beside Kane. "Those fifties will make up for what we lack. Give them a proper bollocking."

They climbed the wall and set up their weapons. Kane had his 416 and Todd his SIG Sauer MCX, which all his commandos were equipped with.

Both men dropped their NVGs into place and could immediately see the multitude of armed figures moving through the darkness. The technicals were still parked in an alley.

"Reaper, are we going to wait for them to get closer?" Axe asked.

Kane pressed his talk button. "Bravo, rules of engagement?"

"You're cleared hot, Reaper," Thurston said.

"Roger that," he acknowledged, then said, "Light them up."

The darkness of the night was suddenly ripped apart by gunfire. Tracer rounds from the fifty-caliber machine gun on the southwest corner reached out like glowing lances burning through flesh with vicious intent. Screams of pain echoed above the *chug-chug* of the heavy machine guns. Kane heard the M249 open up as Axe went to work. Through his NVGs, he could see men fold over like cornstalks cut down in a field.

The first technical pulled out of the alley between two mud-brick houses and the DShK in the back of the pickup opened fire. Heavy-caliber bullets hammered into the HESCO wall; he felt the vibration of each strike as he sighted his 416 on the fast-moving vehicle and opened fire.

5.56 rounds hit at the truck's exterior hard and the driver swerved violently, almost throwing the two men in the rear out onto the hard-packed earth. Kane followed it with his 416 and fired once more, to no effect.

He cursed and stopped. Pressing his transmit button, he said, "Cara, put that technical out of action."

Cara shifted her aim from an insurgent who was crouched near a broken wall to the truck. The CSASS slammed back into her shoulder, and the assistant gunner was tossed violently over the side of the vehicle.

The gunner was to be next, but the Brit commando on the northwest fifty switched his aim and commenced sending large-caliber bullets in the vehicle's direction.

The technical shuddered under each impact, and it suddenly burst into flame. The driver and passenger leapt clear of the still-moving truck, clothes aflame. Cara shot the first man cleanly through the chest. The second insurgent was flailing so much, the first bullet missed. Without a word, Cara fired once more and saw the man drop and lay still, his clothes still burning.

Beside Kane, Todd rattled off round after round at the crouched figures firing their AKs toward them, then moved once more. Insurgents fell, cut down by accurate gunfire, never to rise. The Brit was about to fire at another tango when a machine gun opened up in front of him. Bullets peppered the HESCO wall, forcing the commando to crouch behind its cover.

"Fucking hell." Todd came up, firing at the machine gun position. "Those bastards are serious."

He was about to say something else when Cara's urgent voice came over the comms. "RPG! Southside!"

The south wall went quiet as everyone to a man dropped below the parapet. The rocket-propelled grenade streaked across the open ground and hit the HESCO wall, shaking it to the ground it sat on. A ball of orange rolled up the wall and billowed into the air. Kane felt the heat of the explosion wash over him as he pressed his talk button. "Where is that fucking RPG?" he barked into his comms.

"The wall where the machine gun is," Cara told him.

"Bravo One, Reaper One, over."

"Copy, Reaper One."

"I need an airstrike at these coordinates, danger-close." Kane gave her the coordinates and waited for her reply.

"Roger, Reaper One. We have the target in sight. Keep your heads down."

In several moments, he heard the beautiful words, "Missile inbound."

The star-studded sky overhead was ripped apart as the Hellfire roared in. The explosion was almost deafening and a massive orange fireball leapt skyward, illuminating the area before the compound. The wall, the machine gunner, and the insurgent with the RPG ceased to exist in the blink of an eye.

"That'll make the fuckers think," Todd growled as the last of the explosion faded, but the reprieve was momentary; the attackers picked up their rate of fire.

It proceeded like that for at least five minutes before the fire dropped considerably, eventually petering out. "Check fire! Check fire!" Kane commanded, and the outgoing fire ceased.

Kane studied the scene before him. The bodies of attackers lay on the hard-packed earth, while flames from the burning technical flared in his NVGs. He lifted them away from his eyes and waited for them to adjust.

Leaning back and looking around, he said, "Reaper team, check in."

One by one, they all called in.

Beside him, Todd followed suit with his men. Upon establishing that all were safe, he said to Kane, "That was just a probe, mate."

"Yes. Next time, they'll come at us from two sides."

As though it had heard Kane's words, an SUV burst from an alley and raced toward the main gate. Kane and Todd spun and raised their weapons. "Hold fire," Kane snapped when he saw it wasn't armed. "Just be ready. It could be a suicide bomber to breach the gates."

Along the front wall, all weapons were trained on the vehicle as it roared forward. About halfway to the gate, it turned and started to circle the compound.

"What the fuck is that cock up to?" Todd growled then he realized. "Shit, shoot the fucker!"

His MCX opened up, and the bullets began punching holes in the SUV.

"Open fire!" Kane shouted, and once more outgoing fire rattled along the wall. The SUV lurched to a stop, steam rising from the punctured radiator. All weapons remained trained on it as they waited, watching.

Nothing happened.

Kane lowered his 416 and asked, "What was that?"

"You'll find out in a few minutes. The prick was mapping us."

"What do you mean?" Axe asked.

"Trying to get grid references on the compound for—"

The Brit didn't get any further before the first distant *WHOOMP* sounded and a cry went up from one of the other posts. *"Incoming!"*

Kandahar, Afghanistan

"Someone get a fix on those fucking mortars!" Thurston shouted as the large screen lit up with multiple explosions. Two were near the center of the compound, while three others were close to the building on the east side.

"One of the OPs just took a round," Reynolds said as another explosion appeared on the monitor.

"Damn it! Where are they?"

"I have them," Teller said, his voice calm. "North of the compound amongst the buildings. See?"

Thurston nodded. "Light them up and drop a fucking Viper Strike on them."

"Yes, ma'am," Reynolds replied, then, "Pete, light the son of a bitch up."

"On it."

"Reaper One? Bravo One, over."

"Copy, B—" An explosion drowned him out.

"Say again, Reaper One."

"Sorry. Those assholes are getting serious."

"We've located the mortars, and Pete is painting them for me. Keep your head down. We're sending them the full package."

"Is this going to be loud, Bravo One?"

"Bet your motherfucking ass, it is. Viper Strike. Bravo One out."

Teller glanced sideways at Reynolds. "Bet your mother—"

"Shut up and paint those assholes."

"All done," he replied with a smile.

"Sending," Reynolds said and dropped the laser-guided bomb.

———

Lashkar Gah, Helmand Province, Afghanistan

"Man down! Man down! Northeast OP. Need a medic!"

The voice was British and laced with urgency. Todd said into his comms, "Who is it?"

"It's Gaffer, Toddy. He's fucked up."

"Brick, get over there," Kane ordered as another mortar landed inside the compound.

"On my way."

The chatter of the M249 and the *chug-chug* of the two remaining fifty-calibers could be heard between explosions. The insurgents had begun another attack under cover of the mortar support.

"Reaper One? Bravo One, over."

"Copy, B—" An explosion drowned him out as a round landed close to the wall. Kane felt the heat and earth rain down upon him. He ground his teeth as his anger rose.

"Say again, Reaper One."

"Sorry, those assholes are getting serious."

"We've located the mortars, and Pete is painting them for me. Keep your head down. We're sending them the full package."

"Is this going to be loud, Bravo One?"

"Bet your motherfucking ass it is. Viper Strike. Bravo One out."

"Bet your motherfucking ass?" he muttered to himself. He shook his head and said, "Reaper One to all call signs. Viper Strike is on the way in. I say again, Viper Strike on the way. Keep your heads down."

It seemed like hours, but in fact, it was barely a minute before the laser-guided glide-bomb impacted on top of the mortars. The explosion was deafening and the concussive wave radiated outward, making everything it touched shake. The area around the compound was lit by a massive orange fireball from the blast and the buildings surrounding the impact zone were almost flattened, leaving a mass of dust-covered rubble and flames. As intended, the mortars had been silenced.

Just like that, the attack stopped. The insurgents seemed to melt away, stunned by the terrifying destruction of the bomb that appeared to have been delivered by the hand of God.

Kane said into his comms, "Check ammo and keep an eye out for another attack. Reaper Five, how's our WIA?"

There was no answer.

"Reaper Five?"

Nothing.

"Brick?"

Still nothing.

Kane tapped Todd. "Come with me."

They scrambled down from the HESCO wall and hurried across the compound. "Cara, take over for a moment. Make sure everyone has enough ammo."

"Roger."

They found Brick working on the fallen Brit. The man had taken shrapnel to his left side, left leg, and right thigh. In addition, he appeared to be suffering some kind of head wound. "How's he doing, Brick?" Kane asked his man.

"I'll let you know in a moment. Right now, I'm trying to save his life."

The pair watched as the combat medic put in an IV line and hooked up a bag. Then he grabbed a penlight and checked the unconscious commando's eyes. He sighed, then looked up at Kane. "I am going to need some help if this man is going to live."

"What's going on?" Todd asked, concern for his man evident on his face.

"The leg wounds and that won't kill him, and there's some shrapnel in his right side. That can come out later, but he's got swelling putting pressure on his brain, which needs to be relieved."

"How are you going to do that?" Kane asked.

"I need to drill carefully into his skull without putting it into his brain."

"You can do that?" Todd asked.

"I'll have to if he's going to live. What's his name?"

"Gaffer," Todd told him. "I'll help you."

Brick shook his head. "No. I'll get one of those contractors. You guys need to man the wall. I'll need a medevac too, Reaper."

"Zero, Reaper One, copy?"

"Read you Lima Charlie, Reaper One."

"We need an immediate casevac, priority-one casualty, I say again, we have a priority-one casualty, over."

"I'll do what I can, Reaper."

"Do it yesterday, Luis."

"I'll see what I can do. The whole country is lit up across the board right now. Give me details."

"Brick, give Luis details. I'll go and get you that help," Kane said and hurried toward the building where the contractors were sheltering. "Cara, how're we looking?"

"Clear for the moment."

"Roger."

Kane walked inside and found Mush Thomas sitting with the others near a battery-powered light.

He fixed him with a pointed stare and asked, "You lot all right?"

The man nodded. "Yeah, we're doing OK."

"Good, then come with me."

Thomas climbed to his feet and passed the M17 he held to one of the other workers before following Kane outside. When they arrived where Brick was working on Gaffer, he hesitated a little. Kane saw the expression on his face and said, "Hey, look at me."

Thomas looked at the Team Reaper commander. "Huh?"

"You need to cowboy up right now. Brick and this man need you to put all that shit going through your head to one side and help. Can you do that?"

"Uh, yeah. I think so."

"Leave him with me, Reaper," Brick said. "We'll be all right."

Kane nodded and looked at the destroyed HES-CO gun fortification. The commando had been lucky to survive the blast. He turned to Todd. "You good to go back to the south wall?"

"Sure."

"Good. I'll take the east building with my guy. Send your guy over to the west building where Brick was."

"You know they'll be back, right?" Todd said.

Kane nodded. "Yes. They'll be back sometime. I'm just hoping the medevac chopper will be in and gone before that happens."

"You forgot one thing, old chap," the Brit said.

"Do tell."

"The helo will have to touch down outside the compound because we have fuck-all room inside."

Kane looked at him thoughtfully for a moment. "We'll evac him from up there."

The Team Reaper commander indicated the rooftop where Cara was set up. Todd looked up and said, "Pilot only needs to get one wheel down. Might work."

"Only one way to find out."

"Yes, there is."

———

Kane sat down next to Traynor and let out a long sigh before he lay down on his back and stared at the stars in the cloudless night sky. The desert chill had settled in, and the air was cold. Every breath out formed mist as it was expelled.

"How are you doing, Pete?" he asked Traynor.

"Be better if I weren't here, Reaper. I forgot how cold it gets of a night in the desert."

Kane chuckled. "What would you be doing if you weren't out here with us?"

"I'd be in a bar somewhere, drinking Bud and trying to decide which bargirl I was going to screw."

"Bullshit."

It was Traynor's turn to chuckle. "You're right. An old man like me would be tucked up in bed, snoring my head off. Say, how's that sister of yours doing?"

"Still the same."

Kane's sister, Melanie, was currently in a coma, thanks to a car accident years before that had killed his parents. Since he took command of the operators that would become Team Reaper, she had been secreted away in a care facility in Maine.

"You think she'll ever wake up?"

"Maybe one day. The doc keeps telling me there's no medical reason she shouldn't. She just won't. You got family?"

"Got a sister with a husband and a kid in Bozeman, Montana."

"You never said."

Traynor shook his head. "We don't talk that much. Ever since my parents died, we kind of drifted apart. I guess she's still angry at me for not being there when she needed me most. I was undercover when Ma died, and the same with Pa. The first time, she had Ma to go through it with. The second, she had her husband. Up until then, we'd been close. Not being at either funeral kind of wrecked that."

"I'm sorry, Pete."

"What for?" he grumbled. "Ain't your fault; it's the job. Besides, each time I went home, I'd changed. Couldn't see what I did every day and not let it affect you. But you'd know that. You would have seen it too with each tour you did."

"Yeah," Kane agreed.

"You ever think about getting out?" Traynor

asked. "This time, I mean."

"Once or twice, but there's something about kicking in doors that gets into your blood. Besides, who'd look after you lot if I walked away?"

"I'm sure the general would do that. Sometimes I think she itches to get out in the field and have at it. Is it true what they say about her?"

Kane shrugged and looked at the sky in time to see a shooting star blaze a trail to the west. "I don't know. What do they say?"

"That when she was a Ranger, she led a team onto North Korean soil to recon a missile site."

"Don't believe all you hear, Pete."

It wasn't true. Captain Mary Thurston had led a small recon team into Iran from Iraq to free American prisoners. A helicopter crew had gone down on the wrong side of the border, and Thurston was the closest to the crash scene. She and her team had humped as far as the border before they stopped, unable to go any farther. It was there she had asked for three volunteers.

Every one of her men had stepped forward, so she had to choose. She took her sergeant and two other privates, leaving her lieutenant in charge. They had then walked into Iran and rescued the chopper crew.

Officially she had been reprimanded, but nothing had gone into her record. Unofficially, she was told she'd be promoted and shipped back to the States, which had pissed her off immensely.

"Reaper One? Bravo Three, copy?"

"Read you Lima Charlie, Bravo Three."

"You've got movement on the east and south side. Looks like they're getting ready for another assault. Over."

"Roger. Where's my medevac?"

"Unsure at this time, Reaper."

Now he was angry. "Zero, can you hear me?"

"I'm here, Reaper One."

"Where's my fucking medevac?"

"Working on it, Reaper One."

"Work harder, damn it, before the poor bastard dies."

Thirty seconds after the words had left Kane's mouth, the world around them seemed to fall on their heads.

CHAPTER 3

Lashkar Gah, Helmand Province,
Afghanistan

A booming explosion rocked the night. Outside the HESCO wall, a giant plume of earth rose skyward, and the ground shook. The noise was deafening, and the compound was buffeted by the blast wave.

Suddenly, Kane's comms lit up as his whole team reported in at once. He came to his feet atop the building he shared with Traynor. "What on earth—" the ex-DEA man started.

"They've got artillery," Kane said. "Shit."

Once more, an incoming round ripped through the atmosphere. Kane's voice exploded from his mouth. "Get down!"

The shell landed closer this time, and Kane knew they were walking it forward onto the target. It would take only one or two more before they were right on top of them. "Brick, get your wounded man under cover now!" he shouted into his comms.

"I can't move him," Brick came back.

"Damn it. Zero—"

BOOM!

That one was just outside the west wall, and the force of it moved the HESCO barriers.

"Say again, Reaper One."

"Forget it. Bravo One, copy?"

"Copy, Reaper One," Reynolds replied.

"We've got incoming artillery from the west. Find it before we all wind up dead on the ground."

"Roger that."

"Everybody, make yourselves real fucking small," Kane ordered over the net. "The next one's going to be right on top of us."

The incoming shell hammered the compound yard with shattering force. Wicked slivers of metal, rock, and everything else thrown up by the explosion scythed through the air. Kane opened his mouth just before the explosion so the concussive wave wouldn't blow his eardrums apart. Even so, the sound wave combined with the blast knocked him silly.

Kane's ears rang, and he could taste the dirt and dust in his mouth. He coughed and said into his comms, "Everyone, check in."

One by one, he heard their voices in his ear. All except for Brick. "Brick, check in."

"That was close," his shaking voice came back.

"Get under cover."

"I can't move him."

"Do it. Now."

"Damn it, Reaper."

Kane heard Todd's voice over the comms. "Bull-dog One to Reaper Five, over."

"Go ahead."

"Move him. I'll take responsibility. He's my man, and he would not want you to die along with him."

There was a long pause before Brick said, "Roger that."

"Get him onto the roof with Cara. We'll get the medevac to take him from there when it comes," Kane ordered. He didn't have time to say any more before the next shell came in. That one landed near a building, the roof of which Arenas and Butch, a Brit commando, were lying prone on. The explosion took out the side of it, flinging rubble and debris far and wide. Large chunks of masonry and mud bricks flew in all directions, creating improvised missiles that were dangerous and deadly.

The undamaged portion of the building collapsed, the half-structure unable to support itself now, and took the men on top with it. Kane looked up as the sound gradually petered out and stared through the haze of dust and dirt. He couldn't make out what he was looking at until it materialized through the sifting dust and he realized what it was.

"Carlos! Are you OK?"

Nothing. No answer at all, just deathly silence.

"Come on, buddy, talk to me."

The silence was deafening.

"You'd better speak up, you Mex son of a bitch, or I'm coming over there to whip your ass," Brick snarled into his comms, a hint of apprehension in his voice.

The response was faint and weak, but Arenas' voice was unmistakable. "Man down, *amigo*."

"Shit! Kane swore and came to his feet. "Keep your head down, Pete."

He leapt from the building and landed heavily on his feet. Kane's knees buckled and he rolled before coming up, then he began running toward the destroyed structure. "I'm coming, buddy."

The following shell threw Kane from his feet like a rag doll tossed aside by a petulant child. The Team Reaper commander felt the blast's giant fist punch him in the chest before lifting his boots off the ground and sending him flying across the compound, culminating in a bone-jarring impact as he hit the hard ground. Lights flashed inside his head, and for a moment, Kane thought he'd blacked out.

Once again, he tasted the arid grit of Afghanistan's dirt and dust in his mouth, combined with something else—the coppery taste of blood. With a groan, he rolled over onto his hands and knees, trying to stand up. He managed to get one foot under himself, grunting with the effort, and felt for the 416. He found it and was about to push up when a hand grabbed his tactical vest and said, "Come on, mate. Can't stay out here. Them fuckers are trying to kill us."

It was Todd.

"We've got men down," Kane gasped.

"I heard. Come on."

They moved to the pile of rubble that had been the position of Arenas and the Brit commando. "Carlos, you there?" Kane asked, hoping for an answer.

A moan was all the reply he got, but not one of complaint. Rather, it signified that his man was still alive. Beside him, he heard Todd call, "Butch? Butch! You there, mucker?"

"Carlos, where are you?"

"Over here." The voice was weak, but he heard it.

"Keep talking to me, buddy. I'm coming."

He switched on his penlight and flicked it around the rubble. He found the Mexican buried under large chunks of debris. As luck would have it, his face was the only exposed part of his body, visible through a small opening. "I got you, man," the Team Reaper commander said. Placing the penlight in his teeth, he began moving the rubble aside.

There was a difference between normal triage and battlefield triage. When under fire, normal procedure was to get the casualty to safety before attempting to stabilize. That being the case, Kane intended to do just that.

As he cleared the debris away from his team-mate's body, the light was enough for him to see that

Arenas had been knocked around some. His face was bloody, and parts of his exposed BDUs were torn. His right arm and left leg both had lacerations. What worried Kane most was Carlos' right leg. A large splinter impaled it from front to back.

"Todd—"

WHAM!

The air whooshed from Kane's lungs once more. He got up on all fours amongst the rubble, his mind a whirling eddy of thoughts. Would the next round kill him? Would Carlos succumb to his injuries? Whether they were all going to die in this godforsaken place? He pressed his transmit button and shouted, "Bravo One, have you found that fucking gun yet?"

"Hang in there, Reaper," Reynolds said calmly.

"Hang in there be fucked, Bravo One. We're taking casualties."

"Reaper, what's your status?" Thurston asked in an authoritative voice.

"We've now got three down, Bravo. A priority one, a priority two, and—" He looked at Todd, who'd found his man. A shake of the sergeant's head told him everything. "And one priority four."

"Confirm you have a priority four, Reaper One."

"Affirmative, Bravo. Now find that damned gun before we're all priority four."

———

Kandahar, Afghanistan

The mood in the ops center clearly changed with the report of a dead operator. What was worse, they had no clue as to the identity of the KIA yet. Thurston shifted her gaze and stared at the large screen, watching the feed from the UAV as her people searched frantically for the position of the artillery gun.

Behind her, she could hear Ferrero directing a medevac to Lashkar Gah to extract the wounded. "I understand that, but we've got a situation too. We have people under fire and two WLAs, one of which is a priority-one casualty. If we don't get him out now, he'll die."

There was a lengthy silence from Ferrero before he said, "Thank you," and hung up.

"Give me some good news," Thurston said.

"There's a bird on the way. It'll be there in thirty minutes."

"Let's hope they're all still alive."

"I've got it," Reynolds called. "I found the gun."

Thurston and Ferrero looked at the live feed and saw the artillery piece just as it fired again. "Zoom in," the general demanded.

The camera on the Gray Eagle adjusted, and the field piece came into view. "What is that?" Ferrero asked.

The general studied it for a moment and said, "It's a Towed One Fifty-Five Heavy Howitzer."

"It's one of ours?" Reynolds blurted. "Where would they get one of those?"

"Iraq. When ISIS took over part of the country, the Iraqi troops dropped their weapons and ran. Hell, they got field pieces, armored vehicles, trucks, Humvees… Shit, they even got a couple of tanks."

"We're locked on," Teller said.

Reynolds looked at her screen and said, "Firing."

All eyes were riveted on the monitor, watching, waiting. Then the gun and its crew were obliterated, disappearing in the flash of the Hellfire missile's detonation.

Reynolds said into her comms, "Reaper One, target destroyed."

"Roger that, Bravo One. Thanks."

———————

Lashkar Gah, Helmand Province, Afghanistan

An eerie silence enveloped the compound after the destruction of the artillery piece. Kane looked at Todd and asked, "Can you get a couple of the contractors to help move Carlos to the rooftop?"

"What about his leg wound?"

"The splinter isn't attached to anything, so it'll be just a matter of getting him up to where Brick is."

"I'll find someone."

Kane nodded his thanks and said, "All call signs,

check in."

He heard from everyone except the dead and wounded.

"Reaper One, copy?"

"Go ahead, Zero."

"We've got you a medevac chopper. It should be there within the next twenty minutes."

"Roger."

"Give me a sitrep, Reaper."

Kane let out a long breath. "We've got two WIAs and one KIA. The home team has one of the WIAs and the away team… Well, you can figure it out."

"Yes. How are you for ammunition?"

"We could use some," Kane allowed. "I'll do a check and let you know. Any word on transportation for a civilian exfil?"

"Not yet," Ferrero replied. "I was lucky to get your medevac for you."

"Thanks, Luis."

"Hang in there, Reaper. We'll get you out."

When Todd returned—he had two men in tow to help shift Arenas to the building roof, for Brick to work on him and for extraction—Kane walked across the compound to the south wall, where Axe was still manning the HESCO wall with the 249. "You look like shit, Reaper," he said.

Kane leaned on the wall and lowered his NVGs to look out across the open expanse before him. Bodies, whole and partial, were strewn everywhere from the previous assaults. He lifted the NVGs back up and turned to his friend, rubbing his face. "Thanks. I feel like I've been kicked across the damned country. How are you for ammo?"

"Be needing some soon. How's Carlos?"

"He's out of the fight. He'll be on the bird with the other two."

Axe stared at Kane. "This is fucked."

"Amen to that, brother." The Team Reaper commander reached for his canteen. He unscrewed the cap and took a long drink, then filled his hand and washed his face to get rid of the sand and grit. He offered it to Axe, who shook his head. "I'm all right."

"How's our Godmother doing?" Kane asked Cara over the comms.

"A little shaken, but otherwise, I'm good," she replied. "That arty was something else."

"Can you see anything?"

"Negative. We're clear at the moment."

"Roger. Out."

For the next five minutes, Kane and Axe stood, looking out across the killing field before them in silence. The technical destroyed in the first assault had burned down, and the orange flames were a mere flicker.

Kane looked at the tall building where Brick and Cara were. "Give me an update, Reaper Five."

"Our priority one is stable, and our Mexican friend is bitching like a mother-in-law. He'll be fine."

"Roger. Be advised the medevac will be here in

the next few minutes."

"Good to hear, Reaper."

As if on cue, a female voice came over the comms. "Reaper One, this is Nightingale Six-Two inbound your position for medevac. Advise your status, over."

"Good to hear you, Six-Two. We've got two WIA and a priority four, over."

"Copy. Status of your wounded?"

"A priority one and priority two, over."

"Roger."

Kane went on to tell the pilot what he wanted her to do, and she took a while to answer. "Just a walk in the park, Reaper One. Have them ready to go."

"Understood, Six-Two. Glad you could make it. Be aware this is a hot LZ."

"Aren't they all, Reaper One, aren't they all? Get a strobe on the rooftop when you're ready. Six-Two, out."

"Cara, do you have a strobe?"

"Roger."

"Light it up. Medevac inbound."

A few minutes later, the *WHOP-WHOP-WHOP* of the helicopter became audible, then it emerged out of the darkness—a Sikorsky HH-60M MEDEVAC Black Hawk with its crew of four. It came in from the north and approached the makeshift LZ with a hint of caution.

"All call signs, keep an eye out—"

WHOOSH! The telltale sign of an RPG streaked across the sky, narrowly missing the helicopter.

"RPG!" The call came from one of the British

guys. "It came from the west side."

Kane said, "Get that fifty up and lay some fire down. Six-Two, you're taking fire."

The pilot's voice came back calmly. "Copy, Reaper One. I'd appreciate it if you could take care of it while we're busy."

The Team Reaper commander smiled. This woman had stones. "Already on it, Six-Two."

"Reaper One, we're now taking small arms fire from the east," the pilot came back.

Kane looked at the helicopter as the pilot calmly touched down with its starboard wheel on the roof while the port hung out over the drop to the ground. "Bulldog One, we need suppressing fire to the east, over."

"On it, Reaper," Todd answered.

Out of sight on the far side of the helicopter, Brick and the female crew chief, along with the flight medic, got the two wounded on board first, followed by the body bag with Butch. Then they went to work doing what they do.

Later, on the tarmac, the pilot, Warrant Officer Amy Redpath, and her co-pilot, Laura Kearns, would count no less than twenty-seven bullet strikes on their aircraft.

"Six-Two coming out. Good luck, Reaper One."

"Thanks for your help, Six-Two. Happy travels."

The Black Hawk came clear of the rooftop, picked up its skirts, and with its nose down, flew to the south before circling back around to the north.

When Brick came down from the rooftop, Kane walked over to him. "How were they?"

"The British guy might make it. Carlos is fine, or will be after some R and R. But—"

"What?" Kane asked when he saw the expression on his face.

"He's talking about getting out. He says he's done one mission too many."

"Give him time. He'll come around."

"I'm not too sure. An operator knows when it's time."

"I guess we'll worry about that when he's back on his feet. Get up on the building with Pete. I think those assholes have another attack in them before dawn."

———————

The following morning brought a dull orange sunrise, which spread quickly across the war-torn landscape like molten lava as it rose above the eastern horizon. The expected attack never took place, which was a relief not only for Kane but for all the defenders of the compound. They were bone-tired and took advantage of the downtime to rest.

The reality of their predicament was that they were still penned inside with little food or water, and ammunition stocks were running low. Reports came back from Ops that both wounded men had made it safely to the hospital, and the prognosis for each was good. Help for those trapped within the compound walls, on the other hand, wasn't forthcoming.

"Reaper, you want to come up here?" Cara said over the comms.

"On my way."

"Bring Todd with you."

"You get that, Todd?"

"I won't be far behind you."

A few minutes later, both men stood atop the building with Cara. "What's up?" Kane asked her.

"I think I can see a way out of here," she told him. "To the east there in the alley between the two compounds."

Kane raised his 416 and looked through the scope. At first, he was confused as to what he was looking at before realization dawned that the blue thing was the rear end of a bus. He lowered the carbine. "I wonder if it works?" he mused.

"There's only one way to find out," Cara replied.

Beside them, Todd said, "I have a man who could get it going. Can start anything, he can."

"The problem is going out there and getting it back in here," Kane pointed out.

"Four-man team with Cara on overwatch," the Brit commando suggested. "We wait for them to go to prayer and make our run at it then."

Kane looked at his watch, then raised his carbine to look at the bus again. "We'll have to wait until just after midday. That's when their next one is."

Todd said, "I can't see them attacking us in broad daylight unless we try something. They'll wait until tonight to have another go at us. If we can get that bus, we should be able to roll out of here."

Cara nodded. "I agree. Four-man team. Put Axe and me on the wall and we'll cover you. Plus, we'll be able to cover you with the two remaining fifties."

"Two of mine and two of yours," Todd suggested.

"Sounds like a plan," Kane agreed.

Kandahar, Afghanistan

"The team has a plan," Ferrero told Thurston after he'd finished talking to Kane.

The general could see the uncertainty on his face. "Dare I ask?"

"It's not a—" He stopped.

"What?"

"Let's just say it's a little risky."

"Don't tell me; they've thought up some hairbrained scheme that will likely get them all killed," she growled.

Ferrero called over his shoulder, "Pete, bring up the bus."

"Yes, sir."

The ISR feed zoomed in, and the bus in the tight alley became visible. "What the hell have they gotten themselves into?" Thurston asked, none too happy.

"They're going to get the bus and take it into the

compound. Then they're going to load the civilians onto it and drive out of there."

Thurston shook her head. "I knew I shouldn't have asked."

"Our latest intelligence suggests at least three-hundred insurgents have moved into the city and are concentrated around the compound, completely isolating our team. We can't get to them because all resources are currently tied up with all the other spot fires. This is all we've got. They have to give it a go."

"Brooke, how long will it take to get the Gray Eagle down, rearmed, and back on-station?"

"Three hours, ma'am."

"That coincides with their timeframe," Ferrero told the general.

"And if something happens while it's off-station, they've got nothing they can call on."

"As it is, we've only got one Viper Strike," Ferrero reminded her.

Thurston let out a sigh. Damned if you do and damned if you don't. But losing a team—no, two teams—was far worse, especially if she sat there and waited too long. "Brooke, get the bird down and rearmed."

"Yes, ma'am."

"Get me Kane," Thurston demanded.

"Patching you through," Swift told her.

"Reaper One, this is Bravo. Copy?"

"Reading you Lima Charlie, ma'am," Kane's voice came back over the ops room speakers as well as her headset.

"I've just ordered the UAV back to be rearmed, so you'll be without air support for the next three hours. If anything happens, I'll try to find you something, but—"

"When does anything happen to us?" Kane asked jovially.

"Reaper, this is serious. You people keep your heads down and make a plan to get out on foot if you need it."

They both knew that wasn't going to happen.

"I'll work on it, General."

"You do that."

There was a long silence before Thurston said, "Good luck, Reaper. Bravo out."

She turned to look at Ferrero, and her face said it all. Three hundred against nine and a bunch of civilians were not good odds. "Luis, get me Hank Jones. I'm fucked if I'll stand here and do nothing."

Washington, DC

General Hank Jones, Chairman of the Joint Chiefs, picked up the phone on the second ring and growled, "There's only one person with balls big enough to ring me at this time of the night. What's up, Mary?"

"I need your help, General."

Hank Jones was a big man in his late sixties, and in appearance, he closely resembled Norman Schwarzkopf Jr, or so many of the people who worked for him thought. He was an ex-Special Forces operator who'd started out in Vietnam as a Ranger before making the Armed Forces his career.

"Your people still hung up, Mary?" he asked.

She told him her problem and about the casualties. He listened without interrupting, and when she was finished, he said, "What were they doing, going into a situation like that anyway?"

"We were it, sir. Besides, we weren't to know the whole damned country would catch fire."

Jones sighed. "Yes, we've been getting reports all afternoon. The President is jumping up and down about the ANA. He can sense another damned Iraq coming."

When ISIS first put down roots in Iraq, instead of the Iraqi military standing up to them, they'd abandoned their weapons and run away.

"He's got the One-Oh-One and the First Marine Expeditionary Unit on standby. The Brits and Australians have SAS en route. We're having a meeting tomorrow to finalize everything. Just when we thought things were getting better, this shit blows up."

"I appreciate the fix you're in, sir, but at the moment, my problem is more pressing."

"What can I do for you, Mary?"

"I need to get everyone out of Lashkar Gah," she

told him.

"And you need me to do what, exactly?"

"More shooters wouldn't be amiss."

"Can't do it, I'm afraid," he apologized. "Everything we have in the way of personnel is tied up."

Thurston sighed, and he heard her breath against the mouthpiece. "Kane and the commandos are going to attempt to break out of there. I could use our UAV to open a doorway for them to pass through, but it's not going to be much. You—"

He read her mind. "You want a Ghostrider?"

The AC-130J Ghostrider, one of many AC-130 variants, was relatively new to the Afghanistan theatre of war. This one had a crew of nine and a 30mm GAU-23 automatic side-firing chain gun, a 105mm cannon, and Standoff Precision Guided Munitions that included AGM-176 Griffin laser-guided missiles.

At the other end of the line, Thurston smiled. "A Ghostrider would be fine. Thank you, sir."

"When do you need it by?" Jones asked.

She told him, and he grunted in return. "It'll be there. Take care, Mary."

"Thank you, General."

The call disconnected and she turned to look at Ferrero, who had a curious expression on his face. "Well?" he asked.

"He's getting us a Ghostrider."

"Hot damn."

"Yes, hot-fucking-damn."

CHAPTER 4

Lexington Medical Center, Lexington, Kentucky

Senator Marc Spalding, the fifty-something gray-haired chair of the United States Senate Select Committee on Intelligence, sat rubbing his lined face and black-ringed eyes while waiting in the stark, sterile white hallway of the Lexington Medical Center, waiting for news about his son. Beside him sat his daughter, Rosalie. Like her father, she was tall, had green eyes, and wore a suit. Her long black hair was pulled back in a ponytail, exposing her almost flawless face.

The pair had arrived from Washington by helicopter after receiving the news that Randy had been found by a policeman earlier that evening in an alley with a syringe sticking out of his arm.

Spalding glanced down at his watch, which indicated that it was just after one in the morning. He looked up as a nurse wearing green scrubs walked past with an armful of charts. She gave him a wan smile and kept walking. "How much longer will they be?" he growled.

"Take it easy, Pa," Rosalie said in a soft voice as she took his large hand in hers. "They'll let you know as soon as they know something. Maybe he'll learn this time."

Spalding's daughter worked in Washington for a corporation called Bright Spark Solutions. The name was often confused by people who thought it was a lighting company, not the multi-billion-dollar private military contracting firm it actually was. Rosalie, being an ex-colonel in the United States Army, was head of operations—quite a career achievement for a single woman who'd not long since turned thirty.

The senator raked his daughter with a hostile glare. "Just like your mother used to be. She didn't or wouldn't understand Randy's issues either."

"Leave her out of this, Pa. She's been dead for five years now and can't defend herself. Anything that's befallen Randy has been of his own making. A stint in the military would have straightened his ass out."

"Obdurate as usual. There's no give in you, is there, Rosie?"

"Not when it concerns Randy."

"What if he dies?" Spalding asked fiercely, spittle flying from his lips, his angry eyes orbs of granite.

His daughter withered under his heated outburst, cutting off the response on her lips before she incurred more of his wrath. His words made her realize she hadn't considered the possibility of Randy's death. What if he did die? Regardless of Randy's history of indiscretions, embarrassing the family name, he was still her brother. Instead, she sat in silent contemplation beside her father, awaiting news of her sibling.

A cell phone buzzed and the senator reached into his jacket pocket, retrieving the vibrating iPhone. He checked the screen before answering the call, then poked his finger at the flashing green symbol and spoke gruffly into the device. "Yes?"

Several moments of silence ensued before he said, "It's the same one." Then, "No, just keep an eye on him for the moment."

Spalding ended the call and put the cell away.

"Who was that?" Rosalie asked her father.

"No one."

"That didn't sound like no one."

"It was just an associate of mine," Spalding said with a sigh. "After hearing that Randy had been found, I had this man check into the location of Randy's cocaine source."

"He found out already?"

"He tracked down his dealer."

"Randy's dealer?"

"That's right. He's keeping an eye on him."

Rosalie frowned. "What do you mean, keeping an eye on him?"

"Just that," was her father's terse reply.

Ten minutes passed in uncomfortable silence before the emergency room doctor appeared, the look on his face broadcasting the bad news he was about to convey. The words that he spoke were not necessary but came anyway, "I'm sorry."

Lexington, Kentucky

Orange lights flashed by as her father's SUV sped through the streets toward the outskirts of Lexington. The lack of traffic on the almost-deserted streets made the passage to their destination that much faster.

"Where are we going?" she asked her father once more.

The man beside her seemed oblivious to her presence and failed to answer her question as he stared out the window, consumed by his grief. The driver turned left and then right. The vehicle bumped along an uneven asphalt driveway inflicted with pothole pox, and a large building materialized out of the darkness. Now Rosalie knew where they were. She didn't need the benefit of daylight to tell her.

Even though it was dark, she knew the old warehouse was of red brick construction and towered five stories above them. Each level was marked by a horizontal light-brown brick pattern stretching across the width of the building.

"Why are we here?" she asked as the SUV came to a stop.

Her father looked at her, seemingly startled by her words, as though discovering her presence for the first time since leaving the hospital. His eyes glittered with tears and rage. "This is where it starts."

"Where what starts?" Rosalie asked, uncertain of what was going on.

"Where we start to fight back against the dope pushers, the suppliers, and the damned growers who have infected this country with their insidious products. I have a strategy, Rosalie, but I will need your assistance to make our endeavor succeed."

"What is your plan?" she asked cautiously. "And why do you need me?"

"My position allows me access to a multitude of intelligence. Recently, there has been an upsurge in the quantity of drugs emanating from Colombia. The current hierarchy in government there, unlike its predecessor, has no interest or motivation in reining in production, but rather has harnessed the profits for their own greed, lining their pockets with generous bribes from the cartels. The solution to bringing this monster to its knees is the deployment of American troops to do it by force. But to achieve that end, our government needs to be beaten with a large stick. I intend to do just that."

"You mean, go to war with Colombia?" Rosalie asked incredulously.

"We're already at war, damn it," he snarled. "Will you help or not?"

Her thoughts drifted to the body of her brother lying on a cold slab in the morgue, then to their not-too-distant idyllic childhood before he'd lost his way. Coming out of her reverie, she nodded. "I'll help."

Spalding said, "Good. But make no mistake, Rosie: once you're committed, there's no turning back. Without a doubt, there will be a high associated sacrifice in collateral damage before we're through."

"I understand."

He opened the door of the SUV. "Come with me."

―――――――

Rosalie had met neither the man tied to the chair in the center of the cold brick-walled room nor the man standing beside him.

Spalding crossed to stand in front of the man tied to the chair. Rosalie figured he couldn't be more than twenty-one or -two. Looking up into the face of the senator, the prisoner snarled, "What the fuck you doing? You can't keep me here."

As though he'd heard nothing, the senator told him, "My son is dead." The words came out stilted but were remarkably unemotional.

"Not my problem." Despite the kid's bravado, the look on his face told a different story.

"It is when you were the one who sold him the drugs."

Rosalie looked at the man who stood by. He was broad-shouldered and held himself erect. A short beard wrapped his face in dark hair, but there was something about him that screamed military.

"Prove it, old man."

"I don't have to since I already know."

The senator held out his right hand and the bearded man stepped forward, retrieving a Glock from within his coat and passing it to the outstretched hand.

Rosalie's eyes widened, but they were not as wide as the dealer's. He opened his mouth to speak, but his words were whisked away by the arc of the weapon that crashed into his head, snapping it back.

Spalding turned to his shocked daughter, his eyes now soulless pits, devoid of all emotion. "I want you to assemble a team and be ready to leave for Colombia within the week. I will have Darius here go with you as your second in command."

It took Rosalie a moment to form a response. "That won't be necessary."

"He goes. I want him by your side every step of the way. Nothing can be allowed to stop the plan."

She fixed her eyes on her father. "What exactly is the plan?"

"We're going to manufacture drugs and start a war."

———

Lashkar Gah, Afghanistan

It was time. The four shooters did a final check of their equipment before they stepped out into the unknown. Kane was going to take point, while Brick would bring up their six. Todd would be the second shooter while Fitz, a black-haired commando from Manchester, would slot into the number three position.

"Comms check," Kane said in a clear voice.

"Read you Lima Charlie, Reaper," Cara replied.

"Team comms check."

"Two OK."

"Three OK."

"Four OK."

Kane stared at the big Commando, Fitz. "You're sure you can get this thing started?"

The man smiled. "Bob's your uncle, mate. Besides, if it doesn't start, I'll fucking push it."

"Let's hope it doesn't come to that," Kane replied. "OK, Cara, we're going out."

"Roger. Let her buck."

Kane glanced at Brick, who had a broad smile on his face. "Really, Reaper Two?"

"Oh, come on," Cara came back. "Cheer up. You're doing what you were born to do."

"Just make sure it's not the last thing I ever do."

"Roger that."

"We're moving."

They exited the compound through the main gate

and immediately circled to their left. Sticking close to the HESCO wall, they began sweeping for targets. Upon reaching the east wall, Kane stopped them and said into his comms. "How's it look, Reaper Two?"

"All clear so far, Reaper."

Moving away from the solid surface at his back, Kane stepped briskly across the open ground. Behind him, Todd and Fitz swept left and right while Brick watched their rear. The Team Reaper commander made a beeline for the bus. They crossed a street and then paused at what had once been the mud-brick wall of another compound. A quick sweep to his front and Kane was up again—and just about walked into a hail of 7.62mm rounds from an AK.

"Fuck! Get back!" Kane shouted as he brought his 416 up and let loose in the general direction from which the gunfire had emanated. Taking cover behind the wall, they waited in relative safety as bullets chewed large chunks from it. "Reaper Two, do you have eyes on?"

"Wait one."

Todd's and Fitz's MCXs rattled beside Kane, the gunfire loud as they poured it on. Kane rose and let loose with a sustained burst of his own. Todd called to him, "We need to push on, or we'll never make it. We'll be pinned down."

"Cara," Kane said. "We could use your he—"

"Tango down," cut off his words as the weapon suddenly went silent.

"Move!" Kane snapped, and the four shooters were up and traveling once more.

Ahead of them, another weapon opened fire, forcing Kane into a diving roll onto the hard-packed ground while bullets fizzed and snapped closely past him. Tod stood erect beside him, firing at the attacker, and more silence followed. The Brit commando leaned down and dragged Kane to his feet. "Can't fight or win a war down there, old chap."

"Thanks."

Todd was already gone, pushing forward intrepidly over ground being peppered by bullets—the result of additional weapons opening fire.

"You OK?" Brick asked Kane.

"Yeah. Keep moving."

With Todd and Fitz now ahead of him, Reaper had the opportunity to take a back-seat view and assess the operational professionalism of the two commandos. It was indeed impressive. Fire and move, fire and move. Suppress the enemy, but above all else, keep moving.

Without further delay, they reached the alley that contained the bus and set up a defensive position. Fitz opened the door and moved swiftly into the driver's seat, searching around for the key. After locating it on the floor, he plugged it into the ignition. Taking a deep breath, he turned it, and the motor cranked but failed to catch. Fitz stopped, pumped the gas pedal, and tried again.

Same thing.

"Fuck!"

An insurgent with an AK-47 appeared at the other end of the alley and raised his weapon. With a loud curse, Fitz grabbed his MCX. In a spray of shattered glass and bullets, the front window gave way under the fire from the insurgent's weapon. The Commando brought his rifle around and loosed a savage burst of fire. The Afghani jerked violently under the impact of the rounds and fell to the dusty ground at the end of the alley.

Brick appeared at the open door and looked from the dead man to the Commando. "Having trouble?"

"No fucking shit, Dick Tracey. Keep an eye on the alley, will you?"

Brick nodded and kept his weapon trained on the mouth of the far end of the alley. Fitz tried the ignition again, achieving the same result.

"Rattling piece of shit," he growled and climbed out. He lifted the hood and looked at the dirt- and oil-covered motor, shaking his head. "This is just fucking bollocks, this is."

While Fitz was otherwise occupied beneath the hood, two more shooters appeared, stepping cautiously into the alley. Ever vigilant, Brick was ready for them and dropped both instantly.

While Fitz continued to berate the bus, Kane and Todd were busy laying down fire at a crowd of insurgents that had appeared near them. The latest arrivals were armed with a variety of weapons, but the RPG that was poised to kill on one man's shoulder grabbed their immediate attention.

"Incoming!" Kane cried as the man aimed the weapon and fired.

The projectile cut low across the gap between them, leaving a white tail in its wake. The explosive head smashed into a mud-brick wall to the left of the alley with a resounding *CRUMP!*

Fire and debris shot skyward like an aerial shell on the Fourth of July, and once it reached its zenith, chunks of mud and brick began their graceful rain to earth, no longer resembling the beautiful colors of a descending firework. Kane leaned out to fire at the crowd but was forced back by an insane number of incoming rounds. Todd managed to get off a few shots before he was forced back as well.

"Reaper Two, can you get eyes on that damned RPG?" Kane growled. In the background, the hammering of Axe's SAW told them the ex-recon marine was busy doling out his own brand of fury, his big gun spitting fire at insurgents.

"He's down, Reaper One."

Kane's, "Thank you," was more like a curt "Thank fuck for that." "Fitz, what's happening with the bus?"

"I'm working on it."

"Work faster," Todd snapped.

"If you can fix this pile of shit, be my guest, Bulldog."

"Reaper One, this is Bravo One. You've got multiple groups of bad guys converging on your position. Suggest you get out of there."

"As soon as we catch the bus, Bravo One."

Kane glanced over his shoulder and saw Fitz leaning over the side panel, his head under the hood. "Any time now, Fitz."

The commando, incredulous that nobody seemed to comprehend he couldn't work any faster, pulled his head out and flipped Kane the bird. He then climbed the stairs into the bus and tried to start it again. The old vehicle's motor turned over, kicked, and then died. "You fucking rotten piece of dust-covered shit!" the Commando shouted and came out of the bus like it was on fire. He looked at the ground and noticed a piece of discarded metal lying beside the wall. He picked it up and started pounding on the motor, cursing it for all it was worth.

Hearing the commotion, Kane and Todd looked back and saw the man taking out his fury on the bus. With curious glances, moving their heads back and forth to keep an eye out for tangos, they watched as he climbed back aboard to try again. The engine roared to life, its tailpipe disgorging a black cloud of diesel smoke. Todd looked at Kane with a broad grin. "It's called a knock-o-meter."

Fitz leaned out of the bus door and shouted, "Are you assholes coming or what?!"

One by one, they retreated and climbed onto the bus. With the team aboard, Fitz rammed it into gear with a crunch and it lurched forward. The Commando crunched them once more, going for second gear, double-pumped the clutch, and then forced it home.

The three standing team members grasped for anything solid to help keep them on their feet. They were unable to remain that way for long as a handful of shooters appeared at the mouth of the alley and began firing wildly after the lumbering vehicle.

The back window shattered and bullets cut through the interior, creating eruptions of foam and dust as seats were impacted. Brick rose and sent a long burst streaming out the rear window at the insurgents. The bus reached the end of the alley, and Fitz turned hard left onto a narrow, pot-holed street.

"Fuck, RPG! Look out!"

The three men turned to look back along the street and saw an Afghani standing in the middle, weapon perched menacingly on his shoulder. He pulled the trigger, and the explosive rocket streaked across the gap toward the bus, leaving the man who'd fired it invisible within a cloud of smoke.

Fitz jammed his foot on the brake pedal, bringing the vehicle to an abrupt halt. By some miracle, the weapon's rocket-driven explosive passed harmlessly through the broken front window, along the length of the bus—narrowly avoiding those within—and out the rear window before continuing down the street.

"One of you guys want to shoot that fucker before he tries to kill us again?" Fitz asked casually.

Brick raised his 416 and fired two shots, and as the insurgent fell to the ground, he asked, "Is that good enough for you?"

"Hunky-dory," Fitz came back with as he let out the clutch and started forward once more.

Turning left at the next intersection put them on a new path toward the main compound. As the bus broke into the open, it was peppered with what sounded like hailstones but were a tad more deadly.

Two of the side windows imploded, spraying glass across the aisle. Kane fired at an exposed shooter but missed. He tried to realign his sights, but after a great lurch as the bus hit a pothole, his aim was off again when he squeezed the trigger.

From the driver's seat, he heard Fitz say, "Get the fucking gate open. We're coming in."

The bus bounced hard over something, then lurched to the right. Those within hung on for dear life as the vehicle did the same again in reverse. Then it passed through the gate and into the relative safety of the compound, where Fitz hit the brakes and brought it to a stop.

"Ladies and gentlemen, we've reached our destination." He chuckled.

As soon as the bus had come to a halt, Kane was off. "Cara, how are we looking?"

"We've got hostiles coming at us from the south and the east."

They ran toward the walls. Kane took up position with Axe and Todd with Fitz on the east wall.

"That looked like fun, "Axe growled in between bursts of fire from the SAW. "Can't understand why you wouldn't let me go."

"You'd want to drive," Kane shot back at him.

"So?"

"We all know how you drive."

"That ain't fair. One time I got something wrong, and you hold it against a man for his whole life."

"Just shoot the bad guys, Axe."

"I can't believe—" The rest was drowned out by the chatter of the SAW.

For the next few minutes, the defenders engaged the attackers in a futile firestorm. The insurgents abruptly broke off and faded once more into the cover of the surrounding buildings and compounds. Kane said, "Keep an eye out while we get the civilians loaded." The Team Reaper commander climbed down from the HESCO wall and found his British counterpart. "Let's get these fifty calibers into the Humvees. I'll put Axe in the third Humvee with the SAW. If you're OK with it, I'd like you and Fitz in the bus. He can drive, and you can ride shotgun."

The Commando nodded. "Let's get it done."

They went to work, making preparations to leave. The fifties were put back in the Humvees, their remaining ammunition divided equally, and metal sheeting was collected to reinforce the internal walls of the bus. Once they were ready, all they had to do was wait for their air support.

"Reaper One, this is Ghostrider. Copy?" The voice filling Kane's ear caused a smile to split his face. They'd sent him an AC-130J Ghostrider for air support. Hot-fucking-damn.

"Read you Lima Charlie, Ghostrider. Good to hear your voice."

"You must have friends in high places, Reaper One. We just got pulled off a hot mission to come save your ass."

"I think you'll find this one just as hot, Ghostrider," Kane replied.

"Where do you want it, Reaper One?"

"An east-west run along the front of the compound would do just fine, Ghostrider. Make us a hole."

"Making holes and busting asses is what we do, Reaper One. Hang onto your panties, Ghostrider inbound and cleared hot."

Everyone climbed aboard their allocated vehicles, and the engines were started. In the lead Humvee, Kane manned the fifty, with Cara at the wheel. She edged it up to the open gate and waited. The other vehicles fell in behind her, with Brick and one of the Commandos in the tail-end Humvee behind the bus.

Suddenly, as if the veil of Heaven had been torn, the world around them erupted with a barrage of 105mm shells striking their targets. The earth shook, and Kane could feel the heavy vibrations ripple through the Humvee's floor. "Get ready."

As suddenly as it had started, it was over, and the heavy fire stopped. "Let's go," Kane ordered, and the lead Humvee moved forward. At first, there was nothing. The besiegers seemed to have been stunned into silence by the sudden violence of the skyborne artillery.

Cara floored the pedal, and the Humvee roared. It was halfway to the first block of compounds and houses when they started taking incoming fire. She heard Kane's voice over her comms. "Reaper One is taking fire from the west. I say again, we're taking fire from the west."

The fifty started its *chug-chug* as Kane set about returning the incoming fire. Cara kept her foot down, ignoring the sizzling shells dropping into the vehicle around her as well as pinging off the metal roof. She hit the perimeter and drove through smoke from a fire started by the AC-130. From the rear of the column, she heard Axe say over the net, "We've got technicals on our six. I count three."

Then, "Ghostrider, Reaper One."

"Copy, Reaper One."

"We're going to need you to take care of the three technicals on our six, over."

"Roger, Reaper One. Ghostrider inbound."

Cara swung the Humvee to the left and almost hit a mud-brick wall before she swung it back to the right all to avoid a large hole in the middle of the road. From the rear of the column, she heard rumbling explosions. She checked her side mirror and saw a black and orange cloud rise behind them. More explosions, then, "Reaper One, this is Ghostrider. Your six is now clear."

"Roger, Ghostrider. Thanks for your help."

"We'll remain on station until you're clear of the city."

"Roger, Ghostrider. Reaper One out."

"Good luck. Ghostrider out."

Kane said to Cara. "Floor it, and let's get the hell out of here."

Landstuhl Regional Medical Center, Germany

"Are you sure, *amigo*?" Kane asked Arenas.

The Mexican looked up at his commander and said, "Yes. It's time."

Kane glanced sideways and took in Thurston and the others. The general gave a slight nod. "That's OK, Carlos. I totally understand why you want out. Things have been intensifying lately. A bit hairy at times, and you've got your family to think of."

"I don't want to, but—"

"You don't need to explain. You've fought and bled alongside everyone in this room. There is no justification required, and not one of us will think any less of you."

"Hell," said Brick, "maybe you're the smartest one here."

"Ain't that the truth?" Axe agreed with a weary nod.

"You are family, Carlos. Be assured that we'll take care of you," Thurston impressed upon him.

Carlos swallowed hard, trying to dislodge the burgeoning lump of emotion threatening to break free. His stoic façade returned as he gathered himself before addressing his teammates. "You are all my family."

"Maybe I can find you something to do on Bravo, Carlos," the general proposed. "We could possibly create a position dedicated to planning ops or something similar. You could assist Kane. There is no need for a decision right now. Take time to think about it. Sleep on it, at least."

Arenas nodded. "I will think on it, General."

"Good. Now, let's get out of here."

After the room emptied, Kane remained behind and placed his right hand on his friend's shoulder. "If you need anything, you let me know, Carlos."

"I'll be fine. They are flying me home in a week, and I have my wife to take care of me."

"I'm glad. And seriously, think about the general's offer. I don't know anyone better to help with ops planning."

"I will, *amigo*."

Kane dropped his right hand and offered it to

Arenas, who shook it. "Take care."

"You too."

Kane left the room and found Thurston waiting for him in the stark white hallway. "Is everything all right?"

"Yes, ma'am."

"Do you think he'll take the job?"

"I don't know."

"OK, then I'll ask you this. Do you have anyone in mind who can take his place on the team?"

Kane nodded. "I know someone."

"Who?"

Kane smiled.

Thurston stared at him, waiting for him to speak, her mind ticking over. Then her expression changed, and she said, "No way. Not him."

CHAPTER 5

Outside Junik, Kosovo

"You need to hurry the fuck up, Doc," Raymond "Knocker" Jensen growled, his eyes warily scanning the woods for trouble that could come from any direction. He was nervous, something unusual for the SAS man. Normally cool and calm under fire, the mid-thirties 22 SAS Squadron sergeant with dark hair and beard felt something wasn't right. His senses tingled with anticipation.

He raised his SIG Sauer MCX and swept left and right, looking through the BRAVO5 5x30 mm sights atop the weapon.

In the hole he was digging, the middle-aged man grunted with exertion as he threw another spade full of dark dirt clear. "I'm going as fast as I can, Sergeant," Doctor George Phelps stated.

"Well, dig faster."

Knocker was far from happy. Babysitting a doctor from the UN was not what he'd signed up for, especially in a part of Kosovo that still held dark secrets from the war. That was the reason they were here in the forest: the UN had reports of a possible mass grave where the doctor was currently digging, backed by ground-penetrating radar.

Knocker had been training a small Special Forces team in Ukraine for the government when he'd been pulled back and ordered to escort Phelps on his mission of discovery. Now, in the middle of nowhere in a forest as thick as Central Station at peak hour, Phelps was knee-deep in a hole that was most likely a mass grave.

"Come on, Doc! How much longer?"

"Shouldn't be—" He stopped and bent down to peer into the hole. "I think we've found it."

Knocker lowered the MCX and turned to look at Phelps. In his hands, he held an object stained by dirt from its years of being buried beneath the surface of the earth. The form of the object was unmistakable. "Is that what I think it is?" Knocker asked.

"Yes. It's a human skull."

"Shit."

Phelps sat it on the edge of the hole and reached for the small camera in his pocket. After taking pictures of his grisly find, he picked up the shovel once more and began scraping away the dirt at his feet. Within minutes, more bones and an additional skull sat with the first.

The SAS man walked over, peering down at the macabre objects and noting the holes in the rear of the skulls. No matter their identity, it was clear they'd been executed. "Poor bloody sods."

"I think I have enough, Ray," Phelps said. "We'll bury these items and report back to—"

His words were cut off as the serenity of the woods was rent by the chatter of an AK-47.

Knocker leapt into the hole beside Phelps, pushing the doctor's head below the rim. Bullets showered clumps of dirt on their heads, and the soft earth around them absorbed others while more cracked loudly as they passed close overhead.

The SAS man opened fire with his MCX in the direction from which the bullets were emanating. 5.56 rounds streaked across the open space into the trees. He caught a glimpse of one shooter and laid his sights on him. He fired as soon as they came on, and the attacker disappeared.

A new shooter opened fire, and Knocker felt the burn as a bullet passed close to his ear. The bastards had gotten in behind him too. "Christ!" he hissed and whirled around.

He saw the would-be-killer standing amongst the trees, wearing camouflage BDUs. The AK in his hands rattled again, and the SAS man dropped as deep as he could into the shallow hole.

Beneath him, Phelps cried out in pain. "Sorry, Doc, but those fuckers mean business. I don't think they like you digging around in their backyard."

The bullets from the shooter's AK hit the ground with a *THWACK-THWACK-THWACK!* Knocker rose once more to fire, but a third and then a fourth shooter opened fire, effectively pinning the pair down.

"This is a bit of a cockup, Knocker me old mate. How are we going to get out of here?" the SAS man muttered to himself.

He bobbed back up and fired twice at one shooter, missed, switched his aim, and shot at the next one. That guy went down in a tangle of arms and legs. That left three assholes who wanted to kill him, all because they didn't want anyone digging around in their sandpit.

More gunfire drove him back into the narrow confines of the excavation. There was a dull thud outside the hole, and he stood up to check over the rim. Knocker's eyes widened as he saw what had made the sound. "Fuck! Grenade!"

He ducked just before the thing exploded. The noise was almost deafening, and the explosion created a shower of dirt and debris that rained down into the hole.

"Are you OK, Doc?" he asked Phelps.

"I'm glad I've had all the children I was going to have," he moaned.

"Sorry about that."

More gunfire came in hard and hot. Knocker knew it was going to take a foolhardy action to get them out of their current predicament. He dropped out the partially spent magazine and slapped a fresh one home, then, clenching his teeth, he stood tall.

BAM-BAM! BAM-BAM! "Shit!"

Knocker was too late to get a shot at the third. His SAS training had honed his natural ability and made him good, but not that good. The shooter was going to fire well before he could, and at this range, only a poor shot would miss.

WHACK-WHACK-WHACK!

The shooter jerked violently as rounds hammered into the upper half of his body. He fell to the soft earth of the forest, the weapon spilling from his grasp.

Knocker shifted his aim to where the last shots had come from and saw a man emerge from the trees. He was dressed in jeans and a t-shirt but wore a tactical vest and carried an H&K 416 carbine. His weapon was covering the downed men, and he called, "Knocker, you good?"

"Bleeding heck. Is that you, Reaper?" he asked in disbelief.

"The one and only."

"What did you skive off from to come here and save my sorry ass?"

Kane approached the SAS man. "Maybe we should talk about this later. I saw more tangos back there, and it won't be long before they come kicking in doors."

Knocker didn't need to be told twice. He nodded and looked down at Phelps. "You OK, Doc? Still got your nugget attached to your shoulders?"

"Yes, it's still there," Phelps said as he stood beside Knocker. He looked at Kane. "Thank you, whoever you are."

Knocker chuckled as he climbed out of the hole and helped the doctor out. "Seems you just can't get away from death, Doc. That there is the Reaper."

"What?"

"Not now, Knocker," Kane said. "Let's go. Follow me."

Kane drew his SIG M17 and offered it to Phelps. The doctor shook his head. "You'd be a lot safer if I didn't have it."

Smiling, Kane placed it back into his holster. "Just keep your head down then."

"Oh, I plan to."

They made their way through the trees, using the thick trunks as cover. The forest canopy permitted only filtered light, creating deep gloom in the surrounding landscape.

"How did you know where I was, Reaper?" Knocker asked.

"Your CO."

"Fair enough."

They kept moving until the side of a large dark blue SUV became visible through the trees. As they got closer, it was apparent that it was not alone. They could see two men wearing vests and carrying automatic weapons standing guard over it. Kane held up a fist and stopped in his tracks. Behind him, the others did the same. He waved Knocker forward. "Looks like we've got company. You take the guy on the left, and I'll take the one on the right."

The SAS man raised his carbine and said, "Say when."

Kane raised his 416 and centered his sights on his target. "Ready. Three, two, one, execute."

Both weapons cracked and slammed back into shoulders. The two targets dropped silently to the ground and didn't move.

"Let's go," Kane said.

They hurried forward, doing a full sweep with their weapons, ensuring that they had taken out the only targets, and there were no more waiting in ambush. They reached the SUV, and Kane got behind the wheel while Knocker climbed into the passenger seat. Phelps opened the rear passenger door and, grabbing the panic bar, swung himself into the back. The Team Reaper commander turned the key and said, "What were you two doing out here anyway?"

"Looking for a mass grave," Knocker said. "From the Bosnian war."

"We found it, too," Phelps added.

"I'm guessing whoever was back there was intent on you not finding it?"

"That would be General Milosh Berisha," Phelps said. "Actually, that would be his son. The general is in an invalid home. His son, Besmir, is in charge of everything these days."

"Like what?" Kane asked as he put the SUV into a skid around a sharp turn in the dirt road.

"He runs a branch of the Albanian Mafia."

"And you're out here without backup, digging for war crimes in his backyard. That's fucking crazy."

"Only if you get caught," Knocker countered with a grin.

The smile dropped from the Brit's face as Kane jammed on the brakes and the SUV skidded to a halt at an angle in the middle of the road. About thirty meters ahead of them, another SUV blocked their path. Beside the vehicle stood four men with their AKs aimed at the blue SUV.

"Out!" Kane shouted. "Out now!"

The doors flew open as they tumbled from the vehicle. Kane's 416 came up as he sprayed the blocking SUV with 5.56 rounds. He ducked behind their vehicle and joined Knocker and Phelps. Bullets from the shooters hammered into the side of their SUV, smashing windows and punching holes in the quarter panels. The SAS man said, "I guess your insurance is a dog's dinner. Hope you had a small deductible."

He rose, unleashed four shots at one of the shooters, and saw him fall. The man started to crawl behind his vehicle and Knocker shot him again.

"You sure can pick your friends, Knocker," Kane called to him.

"Not my fault they all love me. Speaking of which, how's that general of yours?"

Kane gave him a weird look. "Are you shitting me?"

"What? A man ain't a camel. Besides, if you ain't noticed, she's hot."

Kane fired again before dropping back down. "That's my commanding officer you're talking about, you know?"

"She isn't mine, though. Did she tell you I met up with her in Dubai a few weeks back?"

Kane's head whipped around. "What the fuck?"

"She wasn't complaining—"

"Shut up, Knocker. I don't want to know."

The SAS man smiled. "All we did was have a drink."

"Thank God for that. Now, how about we finish those assholes off before they call in reinforcements?"

As Knocker slapped a fresh magazine home, he said, "You want to go left or right?"

"Right," Kane replied.

"What are you two doing?" Phelps asked.

"We'll be right back," Kane told him.

Knocker added, "Don't go anywhere."

The pair cleared the bullet-ridden SUV, and true to their word, Kane went right, and Knocker left in flanking movements to open the field of fire. Three shooters hurriedly became two, then one as they took them down with effective shots. The last man suddenly realized he was outgunned and tried to run away. Two rounds slammed into his back and thrust him forward. He skidded to a stop in the dirt, face-down.

"Clear this side," Knocker called to Kane.

"I'm clear too."

"Let's get out of here."

They jogged back to the SUV and stopped short. Their ride looked like a piece of Swiss cheese. "This ain't going anywhere," Kane observed.

He walked to the rear of the vehicle and opened the back, then took out a backpack, reached into a duffel, and tossed several magazines across to the SAS man. "Here. If they don't fit, you'll have some spare ammo. You got a handgun?"

"Nope."

Kane reached back in and took out an M17 in a thigh holster. He tossed it to Knocker and handed him a couple of spare mags. "There."

The Team Reaper commander wasn't finished. He took out a thermite grenade, pulled the pin, and tossed it into the SUV. "All right, let's go."

"Where is it we're going, Reaper?" Knocker asked.

"Home."

––––––––––

Colombia

Twenty men from Bright Spark Solutions dropped into the jungle in the middle of the night, led by Rosalie Spalding and her second in command, Darius. It had been a HAHO (High Altitude High Opening) insertion; they had jumped twenty kilometers from their target and floated in before landing on a drop zone no bigger than fifty meters square. That was the best part about having former Special Operators working for you. The level of professionalism was of the highest degree, and they were perfectionists in everything they did. The alternative was to wind up dead.

They stashed their gear in the jungle before forming up. They were all dressed in black, wore tactical vests and body armor, and had the latest in NVGs attached to their ballistic helmets. Rosalie called two of her men over. Jack Kidd and Terry Maynard were former recon men and had worked in Colombia before. She opened her military Toughbook and hit a couple of keys before a topographical map came up.

"Our target is here," she said, stabbing a finger at the screen. "Jack, you and Terry are our eyes and ears out there. We need to be in position before dawn for the assault. Once you have eyes on our target, radio in. Until then, I want radio silence unless you're compromised in any way. Understood?"

"Yes, ma'am."

"Do it."

Like wraiths in the night, the two men disappeared into the jungle. Darius moved close to her and said, "You should have sent me with them."

Rosalie turned to face him. "Them I know, you I don't. Until I do, you stay with me like my father wanted."

"I'm more than just a bodyguard, ma'am. Use me."

"I will eventually. Until then, you do what I tell you to."

"Roger that."

They traveled through the thick rainforest for the next six hours, then the radio crackled to life. "Lima One-Four to Lima One, over."

"Copy, Lima One-Four," Rosalie said into her comms.

"We've reached the target, over."

"Roger. How does it look?"

"There look to be at least twenty guards onsite, going by heat signatures."

"OK. Hunker down and keep an eye out. Let me know if anything changes. We're about forty-five mikes out."

"Roger that. Lima One-Four out."

———

The sun was coming up when they reached their objective. Rosalie lay on her stomach and looked it over with her binoculars. The target was a drug factory run by one of the lower-level cartels in the rainforest region of Colombia. Once it was captured, her men would cut an LZ into the rainforest that was large enough to accommodate helicopters. After drawing up the plan, she'd spotted a glaring flaw right away. The drug factory belonged to someone, and that someone would not stand aside and let someone else take it over without some kind of fight. So, Rosalie had a drone put up which would—

"Lima One, this is Raptor One, over."

"Go ahead, Raptor One."

"Scimitar Strike is in position and waiting for your go, ma'am."

"Hold, Raptor One."

"Raptor One holding."

"Lima One to all Lima Teams, sitrep?"

"Team Two in position."

"Team Three in position."

"Team Four in position."

Rosalie ordered, "Hold until I give the word."

She gave the scene before her one last perusal. Although the hour was still early, the steaming jungle was causing her to sweat profusely. It ran down her spine and pooled in the curve of her back. Her BDUs were damp as they trekked into position. Rosalie lowered her binoculars and climbed to her feet, then picked up her M4A1 and pressed her comms button. "Lima Teams, move in. Break. Raptor One, you are weapons-free."

As Rosalie's teams moved in to attack the target, the UAV in the air one hundred kilometers away removed the head of the snake.

The four teams moved with the efficiency of a well-oiled machine to eliminate all threats. By the time the firing had ceased, all the targets were down, and the Bright Spark team had sustained neither casualties nor injuries. Rosalie sent out the code words for her success, which were received back in CONUS. Immediately, two C-130s full of men and equipment were dispatched. This was to be the initial drop before the helicopters came—an additional twenty men and everything to make the drug factory better than what it was. Within twenty-four hours, the first phase would be complete. In less than a week, the first batch of poisoned drugs would be headed to the United States.

CHAPTER 6

Worldwide Drug Initiative HQ, El Paso, Texas

"You want me to join your little family?" Knocker asked Thurston incredulously.

She shook her head. "I don't, but Reaper obviously thinks you'll be some kind of asset to us."

"Not even a little bit?" Knocker asked her, forming a small gap between finger and thumb.

"No."

He turned to Kane and smiled. "I see the general still thinks a lot of me."

"Let's get something straight. If you come on board, I'll have none of your shit. If there is, I'll have you out of here so fast your head will spin."

"Yes, ma'am."

Thurston looked at Kane and said, "It's up to the rest of the team."

He nodded.

The SAS man looked around Thurston's office. "Have you people decorated since the last time I was here?"

"Long story. Now get out of here."

The two men left the office, and Kane pulled him up out in the hallway. "You need to rein in your behavior, Knocker. She means every word she says. Understood?"

"Read you loud and clear, old man."

"She was right about one thing, though. Even though I want you in, it's up to the rest of the team."

"Let's find out then, shall we?"

They went to the rec room and found the others there. Cara was reading a book by Clive Cussler, taking a break from her usual war non-fiction. Axe was playing Xbox, while Brick was reading a medical journal.

Traynor, Reynolds, and Teller were there also, the latter sitting next to Axe with a second controller. Reynolds and Traynor were both listening to music.

"OK, listen up," Kane said. All heads swung toward the two men standing just inside the doorway.

Without looking up at first, Axe said, "The Reaper Man cometh." Then he saw Knocker and continued, "Fuck, my head hurts already."

Knocker smiled. "Hello, Axel, old mate. How's it hanging?"

"Don't say a word," Axe snapped. "Don't even speak. My head has only just got straight from the last time I saw you."

Cara smiled and put her book down. She climbed to her feet and walked over to the SAS man. "Hello, Knocker. It's good to see you."

She hugged him and then let him go. He smiled and said, "That's what I like to see, someone who missed old Knocker. It makes his heart swell."

"Hey, Knocker," Brick called. "What brings you here?"

"Well, apparently, someone wants my talent for the team."

The room went quiet, and all eyes turned to Kane. He cleared his throat, then said, "You all know Carlos is standing down from operations and may never come back. That means we have a vacancy on the team that needs filling. I chose Knocker to fill that hole, but it gets put to the vote. Our lives will be in his hands at some stage when we go downrange, and we all need to be comfortable with that. This is your chance to speak up. Let me hear it."

"I say no," Axe blurted. "Sorry, Knocker. You're a good operator, but quite frankly, you do my head in."

"What if I keep it simple for you?" the SAS man asked him

"How about you learn to speak American?"

"I'll go to war with you, Knocker," Cara said. "You're good at what you do. You'll be an asset."

"Thank you, ma'am."

"Brick?" Kane asked.

The ex-SEAL studied the SAS man for a moment

before nodding. "Only if you teach me some of those words you use."

"Done."

"Blimey, what a cockup," Axe growled.

Every head in the room turned to him and smiled. "What are you all looking at? I remember some things."

Kane chuckled. "Looks like you're in, Knocker. Welcome to Team Reaper."

Lexington Kentucky
Ten Days Later

The warehouse rave hadn't kicked off until almost midnight. The DJ had only just finished setting up, and music was not yet pumping.

The supplier for E and other goodies hadn't arrived yet either, but when he did, he wasn't the regular one. This guy had a shaved head and numerous tattoos. When he was trying to get inside, he'd been stopped at the door. , but when he showed the bouncer what his briefcase contained, the guard stepped aside, and he was permitted to enter.

Once inside, however, the supplier was approached by three more men. The guys on either side were larger than the man in the middle. "Who the fuck are you?" he asked.

"I'm the supplier," the man replied.

"No, you ain't. Where's the other guy?"

"He quit."

"The fuck, man?"

"Like I said, he quit. I've taken over his business."

"Why'd he quit?"

"He saw the light."

The three men watched the supplier suspiciously, and for a moment, he thought he might have to pull the Glock tucked into the waistband at his back. Instead, the smaller man said, "Show me."

Suddenly the music exploded to life, causing the supplier to wince. "Here?" he shouted to be heard.

The smaller man waved for him to follow. The supplier fell in behind, and the two bodyguards did the same. They walked around the dancefloor, avoiding the early wave of ravers dancing erratically to the electronic beat, and stopped at the door to a small room. Once inside, one of the bodyguards closed the door, shutting out the bulk of the music, thanks to soundproofing. The smaller man turned to the supplier and said, "Now, show me."

The supplier placed his briefcase on a solid wood desk in the center of the room, unlatched it, and raised the lid. Then he spun it around, revealing its contents to the small man, who stared in silence before raising his gaze, angry at what he saw. "What the fuck is that?"

"Cocaine," the supplier said.

"I can see that," the man hissed. "Where is the fucking ecstasy?"

"We don't deal ecstasy. This is our product. It's worth more money."

"Take it and get out," the smaller man growled. "I will reach out to our old supplier—"

"You could, but you'd need to do it with prayer."

"What?"

"He's dead. So, you see, you deal with us or no one."

"How much can you deliver?"

"My suppliers in Florida can get you however much you want."

The smaller man was silent, deep in thought. Then he spied a tattoo in the shape of a crescent moon on the supplier's forearm. "Tell your boss we can do business."

The supplier nodded and left the briefcase where it was. "I will tell him."

"What about your money?"

"We know where to find you."

After the supplier was gone, one of the bodyguards asked, "What was all that about?"

"Did you see the tattoo?"

"No."

"He had the crescent tattoo."

"So?"

"He is a servant of the Crescent Moon Cartel. They operate out of Florida and Colombia."

"So?" the bodyguard repeated.

"So, you're a fool. Get this shit out there to the customers. And charge them double. If they want to have a good time, they can pay for it."

Two hours later, twenty-seven people were dead from the poisoned cocaine, and a further forty had been affected by it one way or another. Of those, a further ten would die, and fifteen would be left with brain damage. The rest were lucky to have dodged a bullet.

Washington, DC

Senator Marc Spalding watched the newsfeed from his office the next morning with a cold smile on his face. The ticker at the bottom of the feed gave him the statistics from the first strike. Everywhere the camera panned, there were reporters, police, detectives, and paramedics. He even saw a couple of DEA agents.

There were multiple interviews with ravers and a picture of a short man being escorted into a police cruiser by two officers. Then came the inevitable questions: what was the government going to do about it? How many more Americans would die because of the influx of drugs across the border? Would the politicians do more if it were their son or daughter dying?

Spalding turned off the television and walked over to his desk, then picked up the receiver and punched in a number. He waited for the call to be connected and said, "Get me on a flight to Lexington and get a press conference organized."

After hanging up, he headed for the door. It was time for phase three.

———

Lexington, Kentucky

"...and as I stand here and look this camera in front of me, I ask President Jack Carter when the hell he is going to do something about this? How many more lives must be lost to this insidious disease called addiction? While our children die, while our mothers and fathers die, while *Americans* die, this administration does nothing. It is time to declare war on the narco-traffickers, the growers, the distributors—all of them. Put a stop to it once and for all."

Spalding paused his tirade and a reporter called, "Isn't the President already doing all he can?"

The senator fixed his hot stare on the man and said, "Do you really think so? I certainly don't. If he were serious about it, he would bring the countries responsible to task."

"What about the Worldwide Drug Initiative program?" another reporter asked.

"They're good at what they do, Jessie," Spalding acknowledged. "But they are only flea bites on the asses of the cartel leaders."

"They've gotten good results in the past," the reporter called Jessie stated.

"Yes, but it's not enough. We can see that by what happened last night."

"What do you suggest, Senator?" another reporter asked.

"That if the countries who are responsible for harboring these narco-terrorists—that's what they are, terrorists—fail to act, then we, the United States of America, should do so with the full force of our military."

His last words created an uproar from the press contingent, and he stood there smiling. Cameras snapped pictures of him; Spalding could see the headlines now. *The United States Senate Select Committee on Intelligence chair calls for war on narco-terrorists. Wants military action.*

"Senator Spalding?"

His name brought him back to the present, and he stared at a female reporter from Channel 6. "What is it?"

"Senator, does you calling for military intervention have anything to do with the recent death of your son?"

"Damn right, it does. I don't want anyone to go through the pain of losing a child if they don't have to. It's time for the public to rise up and say enough is enough." His gaze went back to the television camera. "Did you hear that, Mister President? Enough is enough."

The White House

"Turn that shit off before I put my foot through the damned thing," President Jack Carter growled to one of his aides, waiting until they'd finished before saying, "Now get out."

Jack Carter was sixty-seven, with a head of steely gray hair. A straight shooter, he often came across as grumpy due to the many pressures of the job, but that was just his demeanor. He was an intensely loyal man, especially to those who reciprocated.

After the departure of the aide, Carter's eyes settled on Hank Jones. "I want you to put your people on this, Hank," he told the general.

"Isn't this a job for local law enforcement? Maybe DEA, at worst?"

"Maybe, but your people have their special means to gain the desired results."

Jones nodded. "OK, then, sir. We'll do it."

"The news cycle has been playing that speech all damned day, and it's starting to get traction. My sources say more and more senators are climbing onto the Spalding wagon. I need this mess fixed before we have more dead people on our hands."

"What exactly do you want them to do, Mister President?"

"What they do best, Hank. Find the suppliers, the

sellers, and most of all, the producers and shut them all down hard. Can they do that?"

"Yes, sir."

"Good. Put them right on it."

Worldwide Drug Initiative HQ, El Paso, Texas

They were all gathered in the briefing room. Being called back from downtime was nothing unusual, and a light buzz echoed around the room as they talked amongst themselves, voicing opinions about what op they'd been recalled for. The door opened and Thurston walked through, followed by Ferrero and Hank Jones. The big man's presence portended something serious.

"Listen up," Thurston told her people. "We have an op that comes directly from the top."

Silence descended upon the room as they waited to hear more. "The general came here straight from the President. He'll tell you what is going on."

"Thank you, Mary," Jones said. He ran his gaze over those before him. "I see we have a new face amongst us."

"Knocker Jensen, sir," the SAS man said by way of introduction. "Late of 22 SAS out of Hereford, sir."

"Glad to have you aboard, son," Jones replied. "Now, let's get to it. I'm almost certain that by now, most of you have seen the news regarding the situation unfolding in Washington."

He paused, allowing Kane to ask, "Is this to do with the poisoning, General?"

"It is, Gunny. President Carter wants it to go away before we end up in a shooting war with some third-world country. That is the last thing we want."

"Is it that bad, General?" Cara asked.

He nodded gravely. "It could very well be. Momentum is gathering amongst the masses to send troops into Colombia to shut down the cartels there. If that happens, you can bet the next thing we'll be doing is crossing the border into Mexico. Before long, the US will be in a full-on shooting war with Central and South America. That can't happen."

"Point us in the right direction and turn us loose, General," Axe said. "I'm getting bored sitting around here anyway."

"I fully intend to, Marine. Mary?"

Thurston stepped forward. "As of right now, we're all on standby. Luis and Pete are leaving in twenty minutes for Lexington, where they'll question the organizer of the rave. Once we have actionable intel, we'll know more. Reaper, make sure your team is ready to deploy at a moment's notice."

"Jungle BDUs, ma'am?"

"More than likely."

"We'll be ready."

"People," Jones said, "a lot is riding on this mission. Good luck."

Lexington, Kentucky

The emotional atmosphere in Lexington was at a fever-pitch. Demonstrators had taken to the streets, demanding justice for all those who'd died from the poisoned cocaine. Vigilante groups were forming to target street sellers, most of whom were armed. To counteract them, the vigilantes began going out likewise. Otherwise-quiet streets were erupting in gun battles, with mass bloodshed ensuing.

The escalation was so rapid that the governor of Kentucky had called out the National Guard, who began patrolling. He was only one step away from declaring martial law.

As the SUV drove past a burning car on its side, Ferrero said, "This is just the start."

Traynor nodded. "Let's hope it can be contained."

The SUV they were traveling in pulled up outside a large office building in downtown Lexington. From the outside, there was nothing remarkable about it, but the basement contained three secret levels that the CIA operated out of. To some, it might seem a little extreme to sequester a drug dealer in such a place, but the authorities were taking no chances, given the number of vigilantes looking for him. The man still had a lot to give.

When they reached the parking garage, a man in a suit was there to greet them. Ferrero and Traynor climbed out, and the man stepped forward. "I'm Wilson," he offered and said no more.

"Looks like things are getting out of hand fast," Ferrero said, referring to the drive in.

"Fucking politicians," the man commented. "Making it hard for all of us."

Ferrero nodded. "I'm Luis, and this is Pete."

"Follow me."

They stepped into a shiny-doored elevator and watched on as the man punched in a code by using the floor numbers. The elevator jerked and began its downward journey.

Moments later it stopped, and the doors parted to reveal a long concrete-and-tile hallway. Their boots echoed with each step as they traversed the cold thoroughfare. They turned a corner and were met by another man standing outside a door who introduced himself as Trent and said nothing else.

The door was opened, and the pair entered an almost sterile room that contained only two chairs, a table, and the man they'd come to see. The door closed, and the man stared at them. "Who the fuck are you?" he snapped. "And where's my lawyer?"

Ferrero sat down opposite him. "I don't know about your lawyer, but I do know that should you desire to see the light of day again, you'll help us out."

"I want my lawyer," the man repeated.

"What's your name?"

"Lawyer."

"Thirty-seven people dead, fifteen with brain damage. You'll need that lawyer, but if you don't want to end up on death row, you'll help."

The man's eyes widened. "Now just hang on—"

"Name!" Traynor barked loud enough to cause the man to jump.

"Pax."

"Where'd you get the drugs, Pax?" Ferrero asked him.

"I can't say."

"Sure, you can. You haven't got a choice."

"I choose not to die, which is what will happen if I talk to you."

Ferrero could see the fear in the man's eyes. "We don't want you to testify or anything like that. Just give us a name."

"What do you mean, I don't have to testify?"

"We're not those kinds of people."

"What kind of people are you?"

"Name."

"I don't know his name," Pax said with a shrug of resignation. "He came into the warehouse with a briefcase full of coke and said he was the new seller."

"He didn't give you a name?"

"No. He didn't even want money for it."

Ferrero glanced at Traynor, who asked, "You didn't pay for it?"

"No. He said he knew where to find me."

"And you have no idea who he was?"

"I don't know his name."

Ferrero saw he was holding something back. "What aren't you telling me?"

"He had a tattoo," Pax said.

"What kind of tattoo."

"A crescent moon."

"Are you saying he was Crescent Moon Cartel?"

"That's exactly what I'm saying."

CHAPTER 7

Worldwide Drug Initiative HQ, El Paso, Texas

"What we have, people, is a quandary," Thurston told her teams. "We've learned from Luis and Pete that the drugs were supplied by the Crescent Moon Cartel."

"What's the quarantine or whatever you called it?" Axe asked. "Damn, I hate big words. Just point me in the right direction and let me shoot someone instead of eating a dictionary and throwing it at me."

The others chuckled.

"The problem, dear Axel, is this." A picture appeared on the big screen and Thurston continued, "Pablo Galvez, the head of the Crescent Moon, along with his lieutenants, was killed almost two weeks ago, which means we can't ask him if he was responsible."

"Who took him out?" Kane asked.

"We're not sure. I reached out to Melissa at the CIA, and she knows nothing either. However, Slick, bring it up."

The display on the large monitor changed and a satellite picture came up. It was gray with pinpricks of light on it. "This here is the cartel's drug factory. Someone is using it, so it's possible that someone else has taken over the cartel. We need to have a look and find out."

"When do we leave?" Kane asked.

"You're not. For this op, we need two teams. Another has to go to Miami to look into the cartel down there. Quite frankly, I don't want to split the team by sending you and two others into Colombia without support."

"Who's going then?" Cara asked.

"I've reached out to an old friend at Fort Benning, and he's agreed to send a team of Rangers into Colombia to have a look around. It'll be a four-man team, equipped and provisioned for a week in the field, after which they'll be extracted."

"I gather you're not sending all of us to Miami, ma'am?" Kane asked.

She shook her head. "No. Just you, Cara, and Brick. Axe and Knocker will stay here."

"Not ready to let me loose yet, ma'am?" the SAS man asked.

"I don't think the wildlife down there is ready for you," she replied deadpan.

Suddenly a cell rang, and Thurston reached into her pocket. She stared at the screen before answering. "Thurston."

There was a lengthy silence before she disconnected and said, "Slick, bring up CNN."

The monitor flashed as it changed, and there it was: a picture of paramedics putting people into ambulances outside of a nightclub in Chicago. The ticker along the bottom told the story. Ten dead and fifteen hospitalized after taking what were reported to be poisoned drugs.

"Damn it," the general growled. "Luis, you and Pete get up there and find out what you can. Reaper, get your ass to Miami. Let's move, people."

Washington, DC

"I would think there would have been more casualties this time around," Spalding said into the encrypted cell he held.

"I can't make them take it, sir," the voice on the other end replied.

"That's fine. It'll give me something to work with. I need you to leave today for the next target."

"So soon, sir?"

"Yes. This will bring the politicians on the fence to the edge. Another incident should tip them over it."

"I'll be in El Paso by tonight and ready by tomorrow."

"Good. Don't let me down."

The line went dead. Spalding was about to put it

away when it buzzed in his hand. "Yes?"

"We have an issue, sir," a new voice said.

"What is it?"

"The WDI, sir. They've been tasked to put a stop to the drug situation."

"When?" Spalding asked.

"Not long after the first incident."

"What?" Spalding almost shouted. "Why am I just finding this out now?"

"I'm sorry, sir, I've only now been made aware of the situation."

"Damnation! Put some people on them. I want to be kept up to date at all times."

"Yes, sir. But there is something else."

The senator sighed. "Of course, there is. What is it?"

"A small force of Rangers is being sent to Colombia to snoop around."

Spalding's anger rose. "Leave it with me, I'll take care of it."

"Yes, sir."

Chicago, Illinois

The Chicago Police Department interrogation room was small, and someone had turned the A/C off, so it was fast becoming stuffy. Ferrero sat across from the woman and stared at her. She was somewhere in her late thirties with long dark hair, breasts that shouted "Augmentation!" and makeup that looked like it had been applied with a trowel.

"Miss—" Ferrero looked at the sheet of paper in front of him. "Callaghan, is it?"

"Where's my lawyer?"

"In good time, Miss Callaghan."

"Do you have any idea who I am?" she demanded.

Ferrero looked up at Traynor. "You want to do the honors?"

The ex-DEA undercover sighed. "Tamara Callaghan. Daughter of Colin Callaghan, boss of the Callaghan crime family. Wanted, oops, suspected of multiple murders, plus drug trafficking, along with money laundering and arms... Shit, do you want me to keep going?"

"Please do," she said, looking into his eyes defiantly.

"Tamara, we know the club is yours, a present from your father. Which also makes you responsible for what goes on within it. That includes all the deaths that took place there."

"You can't pin them on me," she said smoothly. "They took that shit themselves."

"But you supplied it."

"Prove it. Lawyer."

"Maybe we can cut a deal," Ferrero said to her. "Tell us who sold you the drugs, and we'll let you walk."

Tamara snorted derisively. "Yeah, right. You want me to suck your dick while I'm at it?"

"Not with that mouthful of teeth, sweetheart," Traynor shot back at her.

"Fuck you," she hissed.

"My dick would probably shrivel up and fall off."

She grunted in response.

"Tamara, this is the second time multiple people have died from poisoned cocaine," Ferrero pointed out.

"So?"

Ferrero shot to his feet; the chair he'd been sitting on scraped the floor as he did so. "Fuck it. Ten counts of murder coming up."

The two men walked toward the door.

"Wait."

"Why?"

"I'll deal."

"OK. Give me something I can work with, and I'll see what I can do."

"What was the man's name who delivered the drugs?" Ferrero asked.

"I don't know."

"Goodbye, Tamara."

"*Wait!*"

"Come on, Tamara, I haven't got time to dick around all day and night."

"There is a security camera in the club."

"The Chicago PD said they were all wiped."

She licked her lips nervously. "No, there's one in my office. A hidden one. Everything is recorded to a thumb drive hidden behind the picture on the wall."

Ferrero nodded. "All right. We'll go and take a look. If we get what we need, then we'll see what we can do."

They left the room, and once outside in the hallway, Traynor asked, "She ain't getting out of here, right?"

"Not a chance in hell."

"Here it is," Traynor said, holding up the thumb drive. "Just where she said it would be."

The office was large, with a leather sofa against one of the walls. The carpet was dark blue, and there was a large wood desk in the center of the floor. Ferrero pointed at the computer on its polished surface. "Try that."

Traynor sat at the desk in a wheeled office chair. He booted the computer and waited for the screen to flicker to life. "We'll need a password."

Ferrero dug out his cell and punched in a number. He then put it to his ear and waited. It was picked up on the third ring. "Put her on."

There was another moment of silence before Ferrero said, "Computer password."

More silence and then he disconnected. "Everybody wants me 1920. All together."

"Stuck up bitch," Traynor said.

He inserted the drive once the computer was up and opened the folder that popped up. A video started to play, and they could see that it was the room they were in, which was empty. The two men stared at the screen, waiting for something to happen.

"Fast forward it," Ferrero said.

A mouse click, and the feed sped up. Two figures came into the office, a man and a woman. As they watched, the woman approached the man and started rubbing his crotch with her hand. They kissed, then she sank to her knees in front of him.

"I don't think that's our dealer," Ferrero said.

"Gives a whole new meaning to the word 'blow,' don't it?"

"Keep going."

After they got past the cavorting pair, they found what they wanted. Tamara once again entered the office, along with two other men. One was big and strong-looking, while the other carried a silver briefcase.

"This is more like it," Traynor said.

"See if you can get a frame of his face."

It didn't take long. A click, and they had a picture of the man they wanted.

"Get that off to Slick," Ferrero ordered, then took out his phone and hit speed dial. The redheaded tech answered.

"Speak to me."

"Pete's sending you a picture. Run it and see what jumps out at you."

"Leave it with me."

Ferrero disconnected the call and put the cell back into his pocket. "Let's get out of here, Pete.

Bring the drive with you."

They walked back through the club to the front doors. "You want me to get the lights, Luis?"

"No. Leave them."

Once outside, Traynor grabbed Ferrero by the arm. "Luis, wait."

"What is it?"

Traynor ignored the question as his eyes ran over the streetscape. The sun had gone down, and the street was empty. Even the police who had been stationed outside were gone. "Get down!" Traynor shouted as he pushed Ferrero toward the SUV they were driving.

Suppressed automatic fire raked the vehicle they'd taken cover behind. Bullets punched into it, sounding like a wild hailstorm banging on a tin roof.

"What the hell is going on?" Ferrero shouted as the windows started to blow out from the gunfire.

"Someone don't like us," Traynor said, pulling his M17. He rose and fired the weapon four times.

The shooters ripped another burst of fire at them, and he was forced back down. "There's four of them, Luis."

Ferrero fired at a shooter with his own weapon. He dropped back down and said, "We're no good here. They'll pin us and then flank us."

Traynor nodded toward the doorway. "Back inside."

"The door's locked."

"Not for long," the ex-DEA man replied and took off running.

Just before he hit the door, he dropped his shoulder. The door was impacted with so much force, it sprang wide, and he disappeared through.

"That'll work," Ferrero grunted and ran for the safety of the opening.

Bullets kicked up off the sidewalk as they followed him inside. Ferrero dived headlong to the floor and crawled out of the field of fire, then looked around. "You take the bar, Pete, and I'll take the stage over there. When they come in, we'll take them down. Make them come to us."

Taking up positions, they waited for the shooters to enter. It didn't happen in the rush they expected, however, but with the caution of well-trained operators. Ferrero and Traynor were just as vigilant. They waited patiently as the four men crept into the dimly lit room.

The new arrivals were dressed in black and armed with MP5SDs. They also wore tactical vests.

Behind the bar, Traynor waited. He could sense them as they came farther into the club, kind of like a disturbance in the atmosphere. He ticked off a slow ten-count and then came up from behind the bar.

The M17 crashed three times, and the first of the shooters went down as he cried out in pain. From over near the stage, Ferrero did the same, and the shooters were down two. MP5s cut loose, and bullets started to riddle the walls. Behind the bar, three shelves' worth of liquor bottles exploded violently, spraying glass and liquid everywhere.

Traynor flinched as he was covered with the wet stuff and cursed out loud. He stood up, blew off some more shots, and ducked back down.

Meanwhile, Ferrero was regretting not taking the bar. The stage was providing scant cover and just didn't seem high enough with so much lead flying around. He fired at one of the shooters and hit him center mass. The man lurched under the strike but remained upright, his body armor taking the impact.

Ferrero dropped like a stone when he saw the other shooter change his aim and fire at him.

Thus was the mistake made, the shooter leaving himself wide open. Traynor put a bullet in the side of the man's head, and the body slumped to the floor.

Seeing that he was suddenly outnumbered, outgunned, and no longer had the upper hand, the remaining shooter chose flight over fight and made a hasty retreat toward the entrance.

With the exit of the surviving shooter, an eerie silence descended over the club. Both men emerged from their cover. "That was intense," Traynor said, rubbing his hand through his wet hair.

"That's for certain. Get pictures of them, and we'll get out of here before the locals get here. The last thing I want to do is get hung up here with LEOs. Get fingerprints, too."

"On it."

"And check their pockets. I want to know who those sons of bitches are."

Miami, Florida

"Now, this is something I did not expect," Brick said as they drove around the block for the second time. "A drug cartel flying above the radar like this."

"Hiding in plain sight," Cara theorized.

The target building was a mansion in an exclusive gated estate surrounded by many others, all with canal frontage. There was a manned guardhouse on the front gate, as well as security cameras. The grounds were lit with orange light, and the house shone like a Christmas tree.

"This is going to take some doing," Cara observed. "Slick, what can you see on ISR?"

"I count at least six guards, Reaper Two," the computer tech said from the safety of El Paso. "The general also wants me to tell you that Luis and Traynor had some problems tonight in Chicago."

"What kind of problems, Bravo Four?" Kane asked.

"We're still trying to work it out, Reaper. Keep on your toes. This smells like a dead fish."

"Roger that. Can you see a way in?"

Kane turned left to circle the block again, then slowed, pulled over to the curb, and stopped. "Talk to me, Slick."

"I'm working on it, Reaper, but I'm thinking your

best bet is the front gate."

"You've got to be kidding me," Cara moaned.

"Say that again, Bravo Four."

"I said, your best infil looks like the front gate."

"The front gate with the two guards?"

"That's it. I never said it was good."

Kane sighed and glanced at the other two. "Any ideas?"

"We need a distraction," Cara offered.

"Yeah, but what kind?"

"Shit," she growled and climbed out of the SUV.

"What are you doing?"

Unbuttoning her shirt quickly, she peeled it off her arms, revealing a tight white tank top. With several deft moves, she had unhooked and removed her bra from beneath the top without dislodging the stretchy tubing. A combination of the tight fabric and the cool night air did the rest. She tucked her M17 in the back of her jeans and looked at Kane. "Don't say a damned word."

"I wasn't going to. Just wait until you see us come back around before you approach them."

She nodded.

"If I might say—" Brick started.

"No, you may not. Shut up."

Cara closed the door and disappeared into the shadows. Kane said, "Get the four-sixteens ready. As soon as we stop, be ready for anything."

———

Cara strolled casually out of the darkness and headed toward the two guards at the gate. "Hey, boys," she called. "Cool out tonight."

She stepped up onto the sidewalk.

Cara reached behind her back for the M17. Her fingers curled around the butt, and she was about to draw it when her comms lit up. "Stand down! Stand down! The target is cold, I repeat, the target is cold."

The SUV stopped near Cara and she climbed into the vehicle, leaving the two guards with puzzled expressions on their faces.

"What the hell happened?" she hissed as Kane put his foot on the gas.

"I don't know," he growled. "Bravo Four, Whiskey Tango Foxtrot?"

"Sorry, Reaper. Our target just popped up on a camera sweep at a restaurant about five klicks from your present position."

"How the hell did we miss that?"

"It's not an exact science," Swift shot back.

"You're sure he's there?"

"As much as I can be. It don't mean he'll be there when you arrive."

"Send us the address and keep an eye on the joint."

"Will do."

"Son of a bitch."

———————

The Sun Lounge, Miami, Florida

"Are we sure this time, Slick?" Kane asked once more.

"I've not seen any movement. He's in there, along with three guards. You can assume they're carrying."

"OK. Reaper One out."

The three of them climbed out of the SUV. Kane looked at Brick and Cara. "Brick, you clear the place while Cara and I go after Alonzo."

"Roger that."

"Should they start shooting, try not to hit any civilians."

They began moving toward the front entrance. Their target Fernando Alonzo—not to be confused with the Formula One driver—was said to be the Crescent Moon's US man in charge. The DEA had been after him for the past few years, but like Teflon, nothing stuck, so he was still free to roam the streets.

"Bravo Four, do we know if this guy has any surveillance on him?" Cara asked.

Kane glanced at her, and she pointed at a black SUV on the opposite side of the street four cars down.

"Unsure at this time, Reaper Two."

"Well, you'd better find out, because I have a black SUV that screams alphabet soup."

"I'll do what I can."

The three of them stepped onto the sidewalk

and approached the front doors of the Sun Lounge, where a man in a black suit stood guard. He blocked their path. "Do you have a reservation?"

Kane reached into his pocket and took out his identification. "We're coming in."

The man nodded and stepped aside. The three walked past him and through the doors into a dim foyer, where the strong smells of cooked food and air freshener hit them in the face. A well-dressed man behind a reception counter looked up from what he was doing and smiled. "Can I help you?"

Kane nodded. "Show us where Fernando Alonzo is seated."

"The racing car driver?"

"Mister, I am not in the mood for your verbal shit," Kane snapped as he displayed his credentials. "Now, show me where he is and then get everyone out of here."

The man paled. "Su-sure."

He stepped out from behind the polished host station and walked them to a central position where all the diners were visible. Most were eating, but some waiting and drinking. He pointed to a booth toward the back-right corner and said, "You'll find him there."

"OK, now get them all out of here. Quietly."

As the maître d' started speaking to and moving confused diners, the three Team Reaper members wove through the tables until they reached the specified location.

Seated in a plush black leather booth, three men

were tucking into their meals of steak and fries, with varying sauces. Two wore plain black suits and sported goatees, while the third wore a tan suit and was clean-shaven. He was their man. Kane stared at him for a moment before saying, "Fernando Alonzo?"

The diner put his fork down and growled, "Do I look like a fucking racing car driver?"

"Cut the shit. We want to talk to you."

"You the law?"

The two bodyguards' hands lowered slowly toward their coat flaps. "If I were you guys, I'd leave my hands flat on the table before I got a nine-millimeter in the face," Cara growled convincingly.

The hands froze before moving to the tabletop. "That's better."

Kane dug out his credentials once more and showed Alonzo. "There, you've seen mine, now how about I see yours?"

"What do you want?"

Kane nodded at the two bodyguards. "Take a walk."

The pair looked askance at their boss, who inclined his head slightly. They stood up hesitantly before moving away, careful to stay within line of sight.

Kane sat down opposite Alonzo and said, "I want to ask you about a certain batch of drugs that came into the US and is killing everyone who puts it up their nose."

"It ain't nothing to do with us," Alonzo snapped.

"Not what I was told. I have two eyewitnesses

who say that the guy who sold them the juiced product was Crescent Moon."

"Then they lied."

Ignoring him, Kane said, "The thing I couldn't work out is why your people would supply drugs to customers and not take payment for them."

"We wouldn't."

"That's what I thought, too. So, if not you, then who?"

Alonzo shrugged.

"Is it coming from Colombia without your knowledge?"

"Why the fuck should I tell you anything? Huh? You wearing a wire?"

"All we want to do is keep people from dying," Kane assured him. "And if you're not responsible for the killings, I need to find out who is. Can you help me or not?"

The drug dealer stared at him for a moment and then sighed. "We lost contact with the Colombian operation two weeks ago."

"What do you mean?"

"One minute they were there, and the next they were gone."

Kane wondered whether he knew his boss was dead. About to put the question to him, he was interrupted by shouts erupting from outside the doors as four men armed with MP5s barged into the restaurant.

"Gun! Get down!" Cara shouted as she drew her M17.

Beside her, Brick was also moving, and both sought shelter behind a couple of tables.

The MP5s opened up, and a lethal line of lead cut the room in half. Alonzo's bodyguards failed to get their weapons out before they were cut down by the deadly storm. Plates and glasses leapt from the tables as bullets shattered them. Kane took cover beneath the table he and Alonzo were seated at, but the cartel man wasn't quick enough, and a red line was stitched across his chest.

He slumped into his seat before sliding onto the floor.

"Bravo Four, where did those assholes come from?" Kane demanded as he returned fire.

"The SUV outside."

"Thanks for the warning."

"I was trying to establish who they are."

"Now we know; they're here to kill us."

Brick and Cara blew off a magazine each, trying to suppress the shooters. The ex-SEAL got lucky and one of his rounds hit a shooter in the face, taking him out of the fight.

Slugs chewed up everything they touched as the interior of the restaurant turned into a killing zone. Kane dropped out a magazine and slapped home a fresh one before slinging lead back at the shooters. One of them cried out and fell to the floor, followed by another. The final shooter, realizing the tide had turned, backtracked and slipped out the door they'd come in.

The shooting ceased and the three team members came to their feet, weapons still raised just in case. "Clear!" The call echoed around the room.

Kane said, "Brick, check the bodies."

"Copy."

Kane called Cara over. "Get some head shots and send them to Slick. See if we can get an ID on these goons."

She nodded. "On it."

"Reaper One, sitrep," Thurston asked over the comms.

"We've got three bad guys down, and our target is also down. One got away, though. Tell Bravo Four that Cara will be sending pictures through for identification."

"Roger that."

"Hey, Reaper," Brick called. "We've got a problem."

Kane looked in his direction and noticed he was holding something in the air. It took him a moment to work out what it was, and when he did, his shoulders slumped. "Yeah, a big fucking problem."

———

"Say your last again, Reaper One," Thurston requested hesitantly.

"I said, the shooters were US marshals," Kane confirmed.

There was a long silence before the general came

back to him. "Slick just confirmed that on this end. They popped up quicker than an automatic sprinkler head. The question is, why were they there trying to kill you all?"

"Before he was killed, our target said it wasn't them. He repeated things we already knew, so I'm thinking it *wasn't* them. That means someone is masquerading as Crescent Moon."

"But why?"

"That is a good question."

"Another good question is, why did shooters who died three years ago just try to kill Luis and Traynor?"

"Say again."

Thurston briefly informed him of what had happened in Chicago. "Slick just had each of them pop up as deceased."

"This has the damned CIA written all over it," Kane growled.

"I'm about to reach out to Melissa, although I don't think it is. This isn't their style. I don't see them lacing drugs to kill Americans. I'll keep you updated."

"Roger that. Out."

"Reaper, we've got another problem," Cara called as she came through the open doors, her hands raised above her head. Behind her were two uniformed officers, both with guns drawn.

"Shit," he said and raised his own.

CHAPTER 8

The Sun Lounge, Miami, Florida

"Tell me again," the detective in a rumpled suit demanded. He had the look of a man who'd been on the clock for fourteen hours and the temperament to match. All three of the Team Reaper personnel were seated on the curb outside the restaurant, hands cuffed behind them, necks craned up so they could look at the man standing over them.

"We've already told you," Kane repeated. "You've seen our IDs. Now ring our boss, and she'll confirm it for you."

"I will do just that when we get back to the precinct. But before that, I want to hear your story once again. Especially the part where you murdered three United States marshals."

"We didn't fucking murder them, asshole," Brick growled. "They tried to kill us. It was self-defense."

"So you say."

"Damn it—"

"Easy, Brick," Cara soothed. "This guy is only doing his job."

"Well, tell him to ring the general and get confirmation of who we are."

The detective was about to continue when two men in suits approached him. He got a sour look on his face, and Kane could tell there was no love lost for the newcomers. "I was wondering when you would stick your heads out of the drainpipe."

"Now, now, Jim," one of them chided. "Is that any way to speak to old friends?"

"Kiss my ass."

"We'll take them off your hands now."

"You want any notes I have?"

"No, we'll do our own. Take a walk."

"Fuck you. I want my handcuffs back."

Before the detective disappeared with his restraints, the two suits produced their own and cuffed the team's hands in front, then faced Kane and the others. "Serious thing, killing three marshals," the speaker said with a shake of his head. "Real bad for you."

"FBI?" Kane asked.

"Agents Green and Drake," the talker said. "I'm Green. My woolly-headed partner is Drake."

Kane nodded. "Make a call, and this whole mess will be sorted out."

"Really?" Green asked. "From where I'm standing, you're pretty much fucked."

"I have ID in my pocket," Kane said.

"Show me."

Kane gave him his best, "Are you shitting me?" look. The FBI man nodded and reached down, removing the ID from the Team Reaper man's pocket. He flopped it opened and scanned it briefly in the orange light of the streetlamp before forming a disbelieving smile and saying, "What the hell is the Worldwide Drug Initiative?"

"Make the call, and all will be revealed," Cara told him.

"When we get you back for interrogation."

"You're frigging kidding," Brick growled. "Make the damned call. Shit!"

Green turned and waved to two more suited men. They came over, and the FBI agent said, "You take the woman, and we'll take this pair."

Nodding, they helped Cara to her feet, and the others did the same with Kane and Brick. Ushering the group through the police cordon, they made it back to two black government SUVs. As the others were being loaded into the vehicles, Kane spoke quietly. "Bravo, are you getting all this?"

Thurston said, "I'm working on it, Reaper, but no one wants to talk to me. The fact that there are three dead marshals isn't helping. Does anyone know you're in contact with us?"

"Negative."

"OK, we'll keep monitoring you."

Kane was pushed into the back seat of the vehicle, and the two FBI agents climbed in the front before Green started the motor. After checking his mirrors, he put the transmission into drive and sped away from the curb.

"How far are we going?" Kane asked Green.

"About thirty minutes," Drake answered.

"Wow, it speaks," Brick said sarcastically.

"In your ass, tough guy," the FBI agent snapped.

Kane caught the ex-SEAL's eye and shook his head. Brick shrugged and went silent once more. The team leader said, "The detective was asking the wrong questions, you know."

"Really? What should we ask, then?" Green inquired.

"Why four marshals tried to kill us and shot the others who were there."

Green looked at Kane in the mirror. "What do you mean, four? We were told there were only three."

"Four men tried to kill us. Three were marshals, so I'm guessing the fourth was too."

"You're lying."

"Why would I be? And why wouldn't that fourth marshal call the shootout in after he got away?"

Green had no answer to that. Instead, he kept driving.

Six blocks later, everything changed.

A large Volvo garbage truck careened out of a side street in a well-timed run that brought it into contact with the lead FBI SUV. It was a crushing blow that staved in the side, shattering every window in the vehicle and spraying its occupants with flying glass. If it hadn't been for Brick's quick actions in pulling Kane toward him with his cuffed hands, Kane would have taken more impact than he did and been possibly killed when the vehicle rolled. As it was, the Team Reaper commander was stunned and out of the fight for the first minute or so.

Through the ringing of his ears, Kane could hear, "Are you OK? Reaper, are you OK? Talk to me."

Then, "Green, get these fucking handcuffs off us. Give me the keys!"

Eventually, Kane realized that the vehicle was no longer moving and that he was lying amongst glass in the tangled wreckage of the SUV. Through the fog of uncertainty came the pain as everything started to clear.

"What happened?" he moaned.

"Welcome back, cowboy," Brick said, and Kane could feel him fumbling with his cuffed hands. "We've been hit. The SUV behind us is under fire."

Kane's senses started to clear. "Cara?"

"I don't know, man. We need to get out of this shit first."

The Team Reaper commander could now hear gunfire in the background. "Automatic weapons."

Bullets peppered the rear SUV, the thin-skinned panels and windows yielding to the force of the swarms of lead. "Come on, Reaper, we have to get out of here."

They scrambled out of the ruined SUV and crouched behind the upside-down wreck. Green and Drake were returning fire at the shooters but were hopelessly outgunned. Brick said into his comms, "Bravo, we've been hit by two teams of shooters. The convoy is disabled, and Reapers One and Five are cutoff from Two. Copy?"

"Copy, Reaper Five. We'll do what we can to get you some help. Hang in there."

A cry of pain came from Green as he spun and fell to the ground. Blood showed through his clothing where he'd taken a round in the shoulder. Brick hurried over and examined the wound.

"What the hell are you doing?" Green growled. "Get off."

"Shut up. I'm a medic."

Drake blew off half a magazine before sheltering to reload. Kane tapped him on the shoulder. "Where are your spare weapons?"

"Haven't got any," he growled.

Kane's stare hardened. "You can die here or let us help. Your choice."

"In the back," he said as he reached for a key. "Lockbox in the floor."

Kane snatched it from him and, keeping low, went to the rear of the vehicle. He opened the back door and unlocked the box. He found two M4 carbines along with tactical vests and spare ammunition."

As he slipped into a vest, Kane said, "Reaper Two, copy?"

"Copy."

"How you doing?"

"We've got a Feeb down, and the other guy is panicking."

"Did they cut you loose?"

"Why—" There was a pause, then, "Why would they do that?"

"Hold on."

Kane finished slipping into the vest and slapped a magazine into the M4, then scooted to where Brick crouched with Green and handed him the second vest. "Put this on. We're going loud."

The FBI man watched on as the two operators prepared to enter the fray. "You need to cover me so I can get to Cara," Kane said. "They hip-deep in shit."

"Roger that."

"Bravo, this is Reaper One. How's that backup coming along?"

"Five mikes out, Reaper," Thurston informed him.

"Cara ain't got five minutes."

Green asked, "Who are you people?"

"We're the people who get the job done," Kane informed him. "Brick, let's do this."

The ex-SEAL rose and fired a burst at the nearest shooter. He heard Kane shout, "Moving!" and caught sight of the team leader from the corner of his eye as he broke cover.

The M4 in Brick's hands rattled off more rounds, and one of the shooters went down with a howl of pain. With lengthy strides, Kane raced to the second SUV. He had almost reached it when a shooter, unseen by them, emerged from beside the Volvo truck used to disable the first SUV. The man opened fire, and bullets peppered the asphalt around Kane's feet. He dove headlong for the cover of the second vehicle and spun, then let loose a long burst at the shooter, forcing him back.

"Son of a bitch," he gasped.

"What kept you?" Cara asked from where she crouched.

He was about to retort when he saw the bloodied figure of the dead FBI agent. "We've been busy," he eventually said.

He looked at the remaining FBI agent, who was busy reloading. Kane could see the concern in his eyes. "How many of them you got left?"

"Last mag."

"Give me your cuff key."

The FBI agent hesitated before digging into his pocket and throwing the ring to the Team Reaper commander. Kane unlocked Cara's wrists and set her free, but he wasn't done. "The key to the lockbox."

The man hesitated longer this time. *I don't have time for this fucking shit.* "Give me the damned key!"

The agent tossed it to him, and Kane handed it to Cara. "In the back. Lockbox in the floor."

She nodded and hurried to the rear of the SUV as a fresh volley of shots hammered into the vehicle and rocked it on its suspension. When she returned, Kane had just worked his way through his first magazine and was replacing it with a fresh one. "What's the plan?"

Kane edged up and looked through the space that had previously been the passenger window. Then he looked at the truck. "Cover me. I'm going to hook around that truck and see if I can flank the other shooters."

Cara set herself up, then said, "Go."

With the M4 at his shoulder ready to fire, Kane moved quickly toward the truck. He could vaguely sense the bullets from the other shooters cutting through the air around him but ignored them, focusing on the immediate threat.

Another guy emerged from behind the truck, and Kane put two slugs into his chest. The man dropped his weapon and fell to the ground. The shooter writhed in pain, having taken both rounds to his vest, and as Kane stepped past him, he put a round in the man's head.

He walked around the rear of the truck and worked his way toward where the first shooter was.

He said into his comms, "Reaper One, ready."

"Two, ready."

"Five, ready."

"Three, two, one, execute."

Both Cara and Brick stepped up their fire at the shooters in the hope of suppressing them while Kane moved close enough to eliminate the threat. Out in the open, with no cover around him, he held his M4 up to his shoulder. The sights settled on the first shooter, and he shot him twice.

Kane switched his aim to a second shooter and killed him as well. That left one more. He aimed the carbine at him but held his fire. "Hey!"

The shooter spun, startled that he'd been flanked, and Kane shot him center mass, straight into the vest. The man dropped to the ground, stunned and gasping for air. Reaper hurried forward and kicked the discarded weapon out of reach, but the man started to recover, and his hand came to rest on the handgun at his thigh.

"Leave it," Kane ordered.

The man's face curled into a sneer. "Screw you."

He started to pull his weapon, and the Team Reaper commander shot him. "Shit."

As the echoes of gunfire faded, distant sirens wailed in the night. Kane turned to see the others emerge from cover. Cara walked over to him and asked, "Reaper, what the fuck is going on?"

Washington, DC

"What the hell is going on?" Spalding snarled into his cell. "A simple job has turned into anything but. Damn it, am I not paying you enough? Is that it? Do you want more money?"

"Calm down, Marc," the voice on the other end said. "It's just a setback."

"A setback? By now they know—"

"Nothing," the voice cut him off. "They will be so confused at what they're learning, they'll still be chasing their tails."

"I hope you're right."

"What about the Colombian operation?"

"I have informed Rosalie of the Rangers that have been sent to recon the operation."

"I'm sure she will deal with it efficiently," the voice said. "What about our other situation? Have any more come over to our side to support the use of force against Colombia?"

"Yes, but we're still short. I have meetings with more senators tomorrow."

"They need a push. We'll proceed with phase two of our operation. Is there a team in place?"

"Yes."

"Tell them to execute the next part of the plan."

"I'll do it first thing."

"Good. If *it* doesn't get the people of America riled up, nothing will."

"I hope so," Spalding said.

"You'd better, Marc. After all, it was you who brought this on. The rest of us weren't ready to move, but you made it personal instead of looking at the big picture. You see now what happens when things go off-script. It gets messy, and messes need to be cleaned up. I'd hate to see you as part of the mess, Marc."

"All I did was bring it on earlier than planned," Spalding snapped. "War was always the endgame."

"Our endgame, Marc, not yours. Remember that. And remember this: it's our man with your daughter. If this all goes wrong, he will tidy up."

The line went dead, and Spalding lowered the cell and stared at it. The man was right. He *had* let it get out of hand, and if he wasn't careful, he'd be collateral damage.

———

The man on the other end of the call placed the cell in his pocket while looking at the faces of the other three men in his office. One of them asked, "Do you think he understands the gravity of the situation?"

The caller nodded. "I'm sure he does."

One of the others said, "I warned you about using a hothead like Spalding. Now he's jumped the gun and fucked everything up."

"I'm sure it can be contained," the caller replied.

"I hope so. We live in the dark. For us to succeed at what we do, we need to stay there."

The caller nodded. "I agree, which is why, once we have troops committed to the Colombia situation, our associate Senator Spalding will die of natural causes. As you said, he's too much of a hothead."

———

Colombia

"Raven Base? Blackbird One. All Blackbirds down, and we're Charlie Mike."

"Copy, Blackbird One. All birds are down, and you're continuing mission."

The team's drop zone was only a hundred meters square. That made the night insertion tricky but not impossible for these professionals, and every Blackbird hit it on the button. Team leader Master Sergeant Brock Marlin, six-two with a solid build, gathered his team around him in the jungle at the edge of the drop zone. Sergeant Dan Newman was his second, then came Corporals Karl Rand and Ryan Tino.

"Listen up, you guys. You know what's involved. Karl, you're on point. Dan, you pull rear security. Take it steady, and I want no footprints. Understood?"

They moved off through the jungle like wraiths. Each man wore NVGs and body armor, as well as carrying extra ammo and enough rations for the duration. Each was armed with a SIG Sauer MCX, weapons that were in limited use throughout JSOC (Joint Special Operations Command).

Marlin had toyed with the idea of including a sniper on the team, but the density of the jungle kind of limited that idea, so he'd settled on the carbines. They had twelve hours to get on station and set up a lay-up position, after which they would launch their Raven to scout the target.

Marlin checked his watch; it was zero one-thirty. He knew they would be exposed once it became light, but his team was experienced, and he was confident of their abilities.

Around three in the morning, Rand called a halt. Marlin pushed forward and crouched beside his point man. "What's up?"

"Listen?"

The master sergeant listened. At first, all he could hear was the nightlife, the bugs and the occasional night bird, but then it came to him through all the white noise—the sound of running water. "We're near the creek."

"Yeah. You want me to go forward and have a look?"

"Do it."

Rand melted into the jungle while Marlin waited. The master sergeant said into his comms, "Blackbird Two and Four, take five."

The two Rangers acknowledged by breaking

squelch.

Marlin waited and listened to the sounds of the surrounding Colombian jungle, anticipating the return of his man. Five minutes went by, then ten. When it hit fifteen, the master sergeant felt a niggle of concern. He looked around and was about to call the others up when Rand appeared out of the dense green foliage.

"Where the fuck have you been?" Marlin growled softly.

"Looking around."

"You find anything?"

"There's a trail on the other side of the creek, well-worn by the looks of it. Could be for Colombian military patrols, or one of a hundred other reasons."

"Well, we have to cross it. You lead. Once you're on the other side, position yourself so you can cover the rest of us."

"Roger that."

Marlin said into his comms, "Blackbird Two and Four, bring it up."

Within a couple of minutes, the rest of the team joined their sergeant. "We're moving across the creek. There's a trail on the other side. We go one at a time. Move out."

There were about twenty meters of jungle to traverse before they reached the creek bank. Rand was already across when they arrived. Marlin went next. He slid slowly down the bank, and when he reached the water, he tentatively slipped in.

Surprisingly, the water wasn't that cold, but it was deep. In the middle of the creek, some five meters from where he'd entered, the water had reached his chest. The bottom was rocky, and at one point, the master sergeant almost lost his footing, but he flung his arms wide and somehow regained balance. Upon reaching the other bank, he climbed until he made the trail. Marlin paused and listened, then crossed to the other side.

"You OK?" Rand asked him.

"Fine. Let's get the others across."

Tino was next. He slid down the bank and waded into the creek. When he reached the halfway point, Rand's voice stopped further progress when it came over the comms in a harsh whisper. "Hold! Hold! Danger Close!"

Every man froze, Ryan Tino slipped low into the water and waited. Then, "Blackbird, we've got a patrol coming our way. Make yourselves real small."

Marlin eased down into the undergrowth, his heart beating fast. On the other side of the creek, Newman did the same, but Tino remained in the open and was in quite a predicament. He couldn't go forward or back, so he waited.

At first there was nothing, but then out of the darkness came muted voices that grew louder as the patrol approached. In the creek, Tino slipped below the surface, while in the thick jungle off the trail,

Marlin gripped his MCX and waited.

It seemed like an eternity before the patrol finally appeared—six men armed with automatic weapons. As they passed where Marlin was concealed, they joked and laughed. Then they were gone.

Marlin let out a long breath before saying, "All clear."

In the middle of the creek, Tino surfaced and continued toward the bank. Once he was across, Dan Newman performed the crossing without issue. He found Marlin and said, "That was close."

The master sergeant nodded. "Let's hope we don't have any more encounters."

———

The morning dawned hot and steamy, and the jungle humidity soon had the Rangers' BDUs soaked with sweat. With the daylight and the heat came the bugs—little biting, annoying shits that almost drove them crazy.

Marlin said into his comms, "Take five."

Stopping in position, the team sat down, pleased for the break. The master sergeant waved for Newman to join him, and he retrieved a folded map from his pocket. Unfolding the sheet, he smoothed it out and laid it on the ground so it was visible to both men. "I figure we're here," he said, stabbing his finger at a point.

Newman nodded. "About three more hours, maybe four."

"I concur. We'll rest up a few minutes and then push on," Marlin said.

His comrade grunted, and the master sergeant could see something was troubling him. "What is it? Speak up. I'll not have you brooding all the way to the target."

Newman shook his head. "I'm not sure. I just have this feeling, and I can't shake it."

Marlin knew his man well enough not to dismiss his gut feelings out of hand. Trust the gut. More than once, Newman's feelings had saved their asses.

"When we move out, take point."

"Roger that."

"Meanwhile, take a couple of minutes, check your gear, and rehydrate."

Five minutes elapsed before the team got underway again, hitting the trail with Newman on point. The nagging feeling in his gut didn't go away. If anything, it got stronger.

CHAPTER 9

Worldwide Drug Initiative, El Paso, Texas

Every team member was present, gathered in the briefing room in a free-for-all think-tank, bouncing ideas and intel to see what gelled. Having returned from all parts of the continent with their own little snippets of information, each individual contributed to the pool.

Thurston stood at the front of the room with Ferrero. Between them was the whiteboard on which was written all the input. Sometimes a low-tech visual was the only solution to lay out what they had for the benefit of everyone at once, ultimately to help them work things out.

"So, this is what we know," she said out loud. "We have a guy selling poisoned drugs who we are yet to identify. When personnel were sent to investigate both crime scenes, an open attack was made on our resources at each site by whoever is behind this.

The shooters were US marshals or dead people. The cartel we have in the picture, identified by a tattoo on the arm of the seller, has had their leader taken out by—we assume—whoever is manufacturing the poisoned drugs. At the moment, we also have a Ranger team on the ground in Colombia, who should have eyes on the factory in a couple of hours. Am I missing anything so far?"

"The part where the CIA is involved," Axe stated.

"I agree." The general sighed. "It all points to CIA Black Ops. However, unless they have a rogue agent, I don't think they would sanction the mass killings of innocent Americans. Melissa has cleaned a lot of bad apples out since she's been in charge."

"It also doesn't explain the marshals and why they tried to kill us," Cara said.

"What we have here, ladies and gents," Knocker started, "is a dead set conspiracy theory."

Thurston stared at him. "What?"

"You've got drugs—poisoned drugs, that is— coming into the country. Crooked marshals, dead ex-servicemen come back to life, and a dead cartel boss. All of it takes money—a lot of money. They're not afraid to come after us, so that means they have power. You seem convinced that it's not the CIA, so that suggests someone in the private sector."

"You mean, a security contracting firm is behind this?" Traynor asked.

Knocker shook his head. "This is more than your

regular security firm. This is something bigger. I'll bet my left nut that all those bodies disappear—"

"He's right," Swift interrupted.

All eyes in the room swiveled to the redheaded computer tech.

"The bodies never made it to the morgue. They disappeared on the way, trucks and all."

"See?" said the SAS man. "It takes money and power to do shit like that."

"Cleaning up." Kane nodded in agreement.

"But what's the point?" Cara asked. "We already have IDs."

"The better question is," Thurston said, "who are they?"

"They are the Cabal," a new voice answered.

They all stared at the figure in the doorway. The CIA had arrived.

———

CIA Director Melissa Smith was tall and slim, with long black hair tied back in a ponytail. She was in her late thirties and wore a dark pantsuit. As she crossed the room to address the gathering, her heels clacked on the concrete floor with a loud echo. She stopped near Thurston and Ferrero and nodded. "Am I in time?"

Thurston inclined her head. "If you know something we don't, then yes."

Smith faced the room, her brown eyes taking in the people before her. "For the past ten years, the CIA has been hearing whispers about a powerful conglomerate called 'the Cabal.' We believe they come from a broad spectrum of government and private sector agencies—"

"Like the marshals?" Axe interrupted.

Melissa nodded. "To name one of them. We believe they have people in the FBI, DEA, DIA, different branches of the military, the government, judges, lawyers, police departments, and numerous other places we don't even know about. We have barely scratched the surface in uncovering how far their reach goes, but it could be international."

"The CIA?" Kane asked unblinkingly.

"Even the CIA."

No one spoke as they digested the information. Then Ferrero asked, "What is their endgame, do you know?"

"Word is that they have taken to calling themselves the Global Police. They start wars, initiate coups, and bring down governments to suit their needs, or they can influence elections on home soil."

"If you know so much about them, why can't you stop them?" Brick asked.

"Because they work in the shadows," Melissa replied. "They're like wraiths who don't exist, and they disappear in the mist. What this team has accomplished in the past twenty-four hours is unbelievable."

"Wait," Axe said. "Are you telling us the guys Reaper and Luis killed are part of this cabal thing?"

"Yes. I overheard you talking about how much money this would take, and money is one thing they're not short of."

"Still, you guys are the CIA. You guys can find a flea on a dog's ass."

"Believe me, over the past ten years, the CIA has tried. It always comes down to either a dead end or a dead agent, but we believe they've slipped up this time and have been forced to clean house."

"How so?" asked Thurston.

"You've all heard of Senator Marc Spalding?" Melissa asked.

Kane nodded. "He's the guy on the Hill, screaming bloody murder about sending troops into Colombia to bring down the drug cartels. Lost his son recently to a drug overdose."

"Yes."

She waited for their thought processes to catch up. Cara asked, "Do you think he's part of the cabal?"

"It's only a theory at the moment, but yes."

"But why kill innocent Americans?"

"We believe the Cabal wants America to go to war with Colombia. Of course, the government has no intention of sending troops in just to stop the cartels. That's what you guys do. But if the demand for action was so overwhelming that there was no choice—"

"It still doesn't make sense," Kane told Melissa.

"There has to be some other reason."

"There is," said Knocker.

Melissa turned her expectant gaze on the SAS man. "Do tell."

"I was down there twelve months ago with a team, training Colombian military to fight the damned rebel armies they have going on. You know there are shitloads of the fuckers?"

"Stick to the task, Knocker," Thurston reminded him.

"Yes, ma'am. Anyway, I heard whispers of some kind of mining strike said to be worth billions."

Melissa nodded. "It's called trizanthium. You can melt it and make it into body armor for soldiers. It's lightweight and can stop armor-piercing rounds in their tracks. Imagine having US forces outfitted with something like that."

"Like I said, worth billions."

"Is it enough to go to war over?"

"Don't get me wrong," Melissa said. "Sure, they're after the money it can bring, but these guys class themselves as patriots. All for the greater good of America and the world. They foresee a war coming either with China or a resurgent Russia."

"Shit!" Thurston exclaimed. "I hate to say it, but what if they know about our team down in Colombia?"

"Get them out," Melissa snapped. "If you think they're in danger, pull them out now."

Thurston stared at Swift. "Slick?"

"Give me a moment."

He got up and walked to the other side of the room, where a phone sat on a table.

"What do we do now?" Kane wondered out loud.

"We still need to know what is going on down in Colombia," Ferrero said. "We also need to find the man who distributed the drugs."

Thurston thought for a moment. "Reaper, pack your kit. You and your team are going to Colombia."

"Won't they already be alerted?"

"Only to the Rangers. Once we pull them out, they won't be expecting another team. You'll go in dark."

"The CIA has a safe house in Bogota you can work out of," Melissa offered.

"All right," Kane agreed.

"The rest of us will work on finding the main dealer. The Cabal will have to wait. The priority is to stop the poisoned drugs from further distribution on the street. Any questions?"

No one spoke.

"OK—"

"Ma'am, the Rangers are out of their comms window. They won't be back in it for another couple of hours."

"All right. Keep on it. See if there's another bird you can bounce a signal off to get them."

"Yes, ma'am."

"The rest of you, see if you can find that damned target."

Bogota, Colombia

Ambassador Heath Roberts walked out of the air-conditioned building and into the stifling humidity. He immediately removed his suit coat, then climbed into the rear of the armored SUV. The driver turned in his seat and asked, "Back to the embassy, sir?"

"God, yes," Roberts groaned. "Get me out of this heat."

The SUV pulled away, the driver accelerating down the smooth concrete drive from the conference center where the ambassador had addressed young and enthusiastic entrepreneurs about opportunities the United States offered to those willing to work for it. Now all he wanted to do was get back to the embassy, where he could get out of the damned hot suit and enjoy the air-conditioning. A second armored SUV fell in behind it.

The SUV slowed, turning right at the first intersection before traveling four blocks to an intersection normally bustling with traffic. However, this day, there were an unusual number of road repairs being carried out. They slowed and rolled to a stop when a man holding a sign stepped out in front of them. The driver and the security expert riding shotgun exchanged hesitant looks before the driver said, "Check the rooftops."

"What's wrong?" the ambassador asked.

"Evans told me there were no repairs scheduled in the downtown area today in the intel briefing this morning."

"Maybe it was a last—"

"RPG, nine o'clock!"

The ambassador heard nothing since he had no comms, but the two men up front heard every word and reacted instantly. "Mister Ambassador, get down!"

Not questioning the command, Roberts lay across the seat and covered his head with his hands. Outside there was a tremendous roar as a rocket-propelled grenade streaked across the ground and punched into the second SUV. The vehicle exploded in a giant fireball, sending debris and flames across the street and into the rear of the lead SUV. In front of the ambassador's SUV, the man dropped his sign to the ground, produced an MP7, and sprayed the vehicle on full auto. The windshield bore the brunt of the first rounds before starting to splinter. The two bodyguards scrambled for their M4s and tumbled out the doors to return fire.

That, however, was what the attackers had counted on. Two more shooters appeared, both armed with MP7s. They opened fire, and the two bodyguards jerked wildly in a macabre death dance under each bullet strike. Finally dropping to the ground, the men and their weapons were separated in death as the guns clattered noisily on the asphalt.

Abruptly, the shooting stopped. A shocked silence ensued as the two shooters rushed to drag a struggling Ambassador Roberts from the rear seat. They hauled him, feet dragging on the rough asphalt, across the street, tossing him into the back of a waiting van before placing a black hood over his head and leaving the scene of the ambush.

———————

Worldwide Drug Initiative, El Paso, Texas

Ferrero stuck his head into the team room, where they were still making preparations to fly to Colombia, with a grim expression on his face. When Kane noticed him, he asked, "What's up?"

"Everyone in the briefing room, now."

They followed him out and found the others waiting. Melissa Smith was still on location, only this time, she was seated and talking on a cell. Kane and the others stood, waiting to be briefed on what required their presence so urgently.

Thurston started to speak. "An hour ago, the United States Ambassador to Colombia was kidnapped, and his security escort killed. Thirty minutes later, this popped up."

The general stepped aside, and the large screen came to life. A hooded figure seated in a wooden chair took up the majority of the HD smart TV. It was obvious that the individual was male, and putting two and two together, the teams deduced it was the ambassador. The removal of the hood confirmed their suspicions. Judging by the profusion of bruises and blood on his face, Roberts had been beaten. He blinked rapidly as a light was directed at his eyes.

He was flanked by two hooded men, both with tattoos exposed for the benefit of the camera. The one on the left started speaking in Spanish. What followed was a five-minute tirade, the subject of which was America and its law enforcement. It appeared that the hooded individuals placed the blame for the death of their boss squarely at the feet of the US government, and Roberts was about to be sacrificed in revenge.

"Son of a bitch," Kane muttered. "They're Crescent Moon cartel."

The screen went blank. Thurston said, "The ambassador was killed shortly after that point in the stream.

The room was silent as they contemplated what they had just witnessed. Cara broke it by asking, "Is there confirmation of who they are?"

"The tattoos seem to indicate cartel."

"No," Knocker snapped. "No, no, no, no."

"What is it?" Kane asked the SAS man.

"That video was a load of bollocks."

"Explain," Thurston said.

From the corner of his eye, he saw Melissa move to the edge of her seat expectantly. "They were good," he went on. "But old mate cocked it up."

"Go on."

"What are some of the words in Spanish that people—non-native-Spanish-speaking people, that is—fuck up all the time?"

No one answered.

"OK, let me explain further. At one point during that little speech, the wanker who was spouting shit said there would be no *compromiso*. Anyone want to hazard a guess what that means?"

"It's 'compromise,'" Axe stated confidently.

"And therein lies the mistake that so many non-Spanish people make. '*Compromiso*' actually means commitment."

"How do you know this?" Cara asked.

"From my time down there. First thing I fucked up was their language."

"Fucked up your own, too," Axe chimed in.

Melissa finally spoke. "So, you're saying that whoever was doing the talking was not Colombian?"

"Yes."

"And you're certain?"

"As certain as my ass points to the ground."

"It has to be the Cabal," Melissa said. "They're going to use this to go to war. Tip the lawmakers over the edge."

"You have to warn the President," Thurston urged her.

"We've got no evidence, only theories."

"Then I'll go to Hank Jones. Maybe he can do something."

"I hope you're right."

"Make it quick, Mary," General Hank Jones growled. "Things are going ballistic here. I'm about to go into a war meeting with the President."

"It's all bollocks, sir," Mary said, then winced.

"It's what?"

"Sorry, sir. I've been around Knocker too long. The video wasn't made by who you think it was."

There was a sigh from the other end and Jones said, "All right, Mary. You've got five minutes to convince me."

When she was finished, Jones said, "Jesus H. Christ, Mary, I can't take something like that to the President."

"I know it's thin—"

"It's fucking transparent."

"But it all lines up. We're trying to get the Rangers out now. Sir, you have to trust me when I tell you this isn't what it seems."

"Damn it, Mary. I need evidence. Find me some. In the meantime, I'll try to avert a fucking war with Colombia. Christ knows how that is going to happen now."

"I'll do what I can, sir."

"I'm sorry, Mary."

"Yes, sir."

Thurston hung up and went back to the briefing room, finding the others still there. All eyes locked on her expectantly. Kane asked, "What do we do, General?"

"We continue the mission. Reaper, take your team to Colombia. Melissa, can we get help from you and your people?"

"Just tell me what you need."

"The rest of us need to find that distributor. Our top priority is stopping the flow of poisoned drugs. We do that, and we stop a war. The Cabal comes second. It'll take us too long to get the evidence we need. I just hope we find some as we go. Once we finish here, I'll reach out to Admiral Joseph and see if he can keep a team on standby for us just in case. Make no mistake, people, we're about to go onto a war footing, and you'll be in the middle of the hostilities. Stay safe."

"Ma'am, what exactly did General Jones say?"

"He said, 'Good luck.'"

The White House, Washington, DC

As Hank Jones walked down the hall, a naval officer attired in dress whites fell in beside him, their footsteps echoing as one. "I just heard from Mary Thurston. She asked whether I could put Scimitar on standby for her."

"What did you say, Joe?"

Rear Admiral Alexander Joseph was the commander of the United States Naval Special Warfare Command (NAVSPECWARCOM). He'd helped the team on several occasions when things were tight. He was also a close friend of Hank Jones'. "I told her I'd see what I could do. Although I doubt it will be anything. I think we'll be on a war footing by the end of the day, and all my spare teams will be on standby to deploy. She did say something strange, though."

Jones stopped and took the admiral to one side, where they were out of the way. "What, Joe?"

"She told me not to tell anyone. You know why she would want that?"

Jones sighed. There was no avoiding it. "What I'm about to tell you stays between you and me. OK?"

The admiral nodded. "You got it, Hank."

When the general was finished, Joseph nodded and said, "OK, I'll hold Hunt and his men back, but I can't do it indefinitely. At some stage, I'll have to deploy them."

"I know. I'm recommending that we deploy the USS *Jackson* Task Group and the First, Fifth, and Seventh Marine Regiments to start with."

"Shit, Hank. Don't you want to stop this before it starts if what you tell me is true?"

"Of course, I do, Joe. But I'll be asked for a recommendation, and that will be it. I'll see if I can get a word with the President after we're done. I just hope nothing else goes to shit before we can get on top of this thing."

———————

With the meeting finished, the two men hung back to speak to the President. He waited for the door to close and said, "All right, what is it?"

Jones said, "I caution you against any armed conflict with Colombia, sir."

Carter stared at him for a moment before he spoke. "Why?"

"Because it might not be as it seems, sir."

"You just advised me to send a carrier group and three Marine regiments down there. Joe is going to deploy SEAL teams within the next twenty-four hours, and now you tell me that I shouldn't. So, again, I ask why?"

"The team is working on something, Mister President. It's quite possible that there are outside forces interfering in this."

"What forces, damn it?" Carter demanded. "They're killing innocent Americans. The public is furious, as are both the Dems and Republicans. We're about an inch away from going to war."

"They're still working on getting evidence, sir. What they *have* come up with is that the death of the Crescent Moon cartel's boss, the drugs, and the assassination of the ambassador are all connected and were effectuated by the same people."

"Then find out who. Nothing changes, got it?"

Jones could have elaborated but realized that prudence should prevail. There was no point without solid evidence. He was about to speak when Carter looked at him thoughtfully. "What aren't you telling me, Hank?"

"Sir?"

"We've known each other for years, Hank. I can discern when you're holding back."

Jones glanced at Joseph, who shrugged. "Good luck."

"Come on, Hank. Out with it."

Jones sighed and briefly considered whether what he was about to reveal would cast him as a fool. "There are reports that the ones behind all this are a secret cabal of powerful people from within our borders, sir."

For a moment, Carter was silent, and Jones fully expected him to start laughing. Instead, he said in a level voice, "Is there any truth to those reports, Hank?"

"We're trying to ascertain that as we speak, sir. One thing Mary and her people are sure of is that it was not Colombians behind the atrocities."

Carter maintained his silence.

Joseph cleared his throat and said, "If you don't mind me saying so, sir, you don't seem surprised."

Carter fixed him with a steady gaze and said, "There have always been rumors about a cabal. It became something of an urban legend. Of course, they have been waved off as talk and nothing more, but it never seemed to go away. How did your people come across this whole cabal thing anyway?"

"In Chicago, some of them were targeted by a hit team of dead men, and in Miami, US Marshals tried to kill Kane and a few others. They thought it smacked of CIA. Melissa Smith flew down to El Paso to clarify things," Jones explained.

"So that was why her deputy was standing in for her."

"Yes, sir.

"All right, I will stall as long as I can, but if you don't come up with something concrete soon, I can't help you."

"I'll let them know, sir."

"Good luck. And for all our sakes, I hope this isn't a damned ghost hunt. A decision to go to war isn't made lightly."

Washington, DC

Marc Spalding took the cell from his pocket and punched in a number. He waited as the connection was made. On the fourth ring, it was answered. "Yes?"

"It worked. The President has ordered the *Jackson* Carrier Group to sea and the First, Fifth, and Seventh Marines with it."

"Good. What about our other problem?"

"No news."

There was a long silence, and Spalding pictured

the man on the other end considering his next words. Then, "Recall the team in Colombia. Have them destroy the drug factory. It has outlived its usefulness, and we don't need it anymore."

"I'll send word."

"Good. I want you to tidy up the loose ends before they get tracked down. The distributor. The team we used for the ambassador."

"I'll see to it."

The line went dead.

Spalding looked at the cell and thought for a moment, then punched in another number and waited for the person on the other end to answer. "Yes?"

"Time to do the next one."

"I'll get it done."

CHAPTER 10

Colombia

"We've been ordered out," Newman told his commander. "Word just came through. Our mission is compromised."

"Shit. All right, call the others in."

Newman spoke into his comms and waited for the other two to acknowledge. "This is a damned clusterfuck, Brock."

"Yes. The sooner we get out—" He stopped.

Newman saw the expression on his face and asked, "What is it?"

"Listen."

They both listened in silence, Newman trying to work out what Marlin had heard. Then he realized it was what he didn't hear. Everything was quiet; not a bug, bird, or any type of animal made a sound. He gripped his MCX and scanned the deep green of the thick, leafy jungle. A bead of sweat rolled down the Newman's camouflage-painted face and he licked his lips, but his tongue was dry. He always got that way when the shit was about—

The jungle around them lit up. The air came alive with angry lead hornets that scythed through the thick foliage and laid it out like a carpet. Beside Newman, Marlin's head snapped to one side as two rounds hammered into his face and throat.

"Fuck!" Newman exclaimed and dove to the ground, opening fire with his MCX. "Everyone scatter, acknowledge," he barked into his comms.

There was no reply, and Newman tried again. Still nothing except the rattle and snap of gunfire. "Damn it! Raven Base, this is Blackbird Two. We're taking fire and my team is down, over."

The crackle of static fed back through his comms, so the Ranger tried again. "Raven Base, this is Blackbird Two, do you read? Over?"

"Go ahead, Blackbird Two."

"Raven—" Gunfire cut close and made Newman hug the ground. "Raven Base, I'm declaring an emergency. All call signs are down except for me. Taking heavy fire."

"Roger, Blackbird. Put your E&E into practice, over."

"Copy, will escape and evade."

"Good luck, Blackbird."

"Yeah, I'll fucking need it," Newman muttered to himself. He slid backward through the undergrowth and disappeared behind a thick green clump. Rounds trimmed leaves from the jungle growth but soon came to a halt, permitting the Ranger to slither away. His heart was heavy at the thought of leaving his teammates behind, but he knew his survival was paramount, and it hinged on getting away from the killing field. Once clear, he would radio in and let them know. From there, it was anyone's guess what came next.

Worldwide Drug Initiative, El Paso, Texas

"Reaper, you have to go now," Thurston said urgently. "The Ranger team just got hit in Colombia, and we've got three men down and one working an E&E pattern."

"We're more or less ready to go, General," Kane told her. "The rest we can do on the plane."

"Good. Wheels up in thirty minutes."

Kane and the others grabbed their kits and hurried out to the two SUVs that would transport them to the waiting C-17. Once they were on the road, Kane reached out to the HQ. "What can you tell us, ma'am?"

"Thirty minutes ago, the Rangers got hit by an unknown aggressor. Three of them are assumed KIA, with one on the run. His call sign is Blackbird Two. His real name is Sergeant Dan Newman. He's currently working an E&E pattern, trying to lose the attackers. Reaper Team will jump into the jungle five klicks to the west of the target area. That should put you on an intercept course with Blackbird. Once you're down, you'll proceed east. If there's any more, I'll update you in the air."

"What backup will we have?"

"Scimitar and his team are on standby. If you need air support, don't hold your breath. Once you're in the jungle, the only firepower is whatever weapons you carry with you."

"Understood."

"Once you have Blackbird, you'll have to make your way to Bogota by any means you can. Did you get the memo about no BDUs?"

"Yes."

"Good. The less you look like soldiers, the better off you'll be if you get picked up."

"Don't they shoot mercenaries in Colombia, ma'am?"

"Minor technicality. Good luck."

"Yes, ma'am."

They arrived at the base with ten minutes to spare, loaded the C-17 with what they had with them, and were wheels up right on time. Now all they could do was wait.

———

Phoenix, Arizona

A silver Audi sat outside the loft nightclub, the man

with the tattoos watching people come and go. All the patrons appeared to be middle-aged couples, which was to be expected since the nightclub was a favorite haunt for swinging couples. They hooked up there and then left with the person or people they wanted to explore their particular proclivities with. When he figured the time was right, he climbed out of the vehicle and walked toward the front entrance.

Standing at the door was a tall, thin man wearing a leather jacket. He looked down at the briefcase and then back up. "Who are you?"

"I'm the party man," the supplier said, holding up the briefcase.

The security guard shook his head and said, "No, you ain't."

The man reached into his pocket and took out a five-hundred-dollar roll of notes. "Yes, I am."

After staring at the cash for several moments, the decision was a no-brainer for the security guard, who reached out to accept it. "Yeah, I guess you are."

The supplier walked inside and climbed the stairs.

At the top, another door opened, admitting him to a medium-sized room where mood lighting created an intimate ambiance for the benefit of the establishment's patrons.

The supplier looked around, taking in everything before him. Couples sat in booths, at tables, or at the bar, talking quietly, sipping drinks and getting to know each other. In a booth at the back of the room, two couples seemed to be enjoying each other's company. While the supplier watched, the man from one couple took the hand of the woman from the other couple and led her toward a nearby door, leaving their respective partners at the table. The woman rose from her seat and moved around to slide into the booth beside the man, never once taking her eyes from his. She placed her hand beneath the table, and he could see her bare shoulder move where her red dress hung down. When she leaned close to the man's face, her long hair swung down like a sheet, obscuring the distributor's view of proceedings. He assumed that she was kissing the man long and passionately. A few moments later, the hair swung back behind her shoulders, and the pair rose from the booth and followed the other two.

"Hey, what you got in the briefcase?" a customer asked, snapping him back to attention.

The supplier looked at the man and said, "Samples."

The customer raised his eyebrows. "Really?"

"Sure."

"Can I sample one?"

"Here?"

The customer shook his head. "Nah, we'll go into the other room. They'll all be too busy fucking to notice."

"Lead on."

The customer was accurate in his assessment of the goings-on. As soon as the door swung open, the supplier could smell the heavy scent of sex. Nearly everyone in the room was naked. Cries of passion and animalistic grunting echoed throughout the space as stark-white butts pumped and thrust. At a table in the corner, he saw a couple doing lines and smiled. This would do. He placed the briefcase on a table and flipped the latches. When he opened the case to display the contents, the eyes of the man with the supplier lit up in anticipation. "Can I try?"

"Like I said, they're samples."

"Holy fuck, dude."

A woman noticed the candy display and walked to where they stood, hips swaying, breasts unmoving because of her implants. She looked at the supplier and asked, "Who do I have to blow to get some of this shit?"

The supplier returned her smile and said, "As much fun as that sounds, no one."

"You sure?" she asked. "I'm ready to screw someone else tonight. It might as well be you."

Ever so slowly, people in various stages of undress drifted over, took samples, and retreated to whence they had come. Before long, many were occupied with the drugs or in the state induced by the drugs, and they failed to notice the departure of the supplier.

That night, eighteen swingers died, and another seven went to the emergency room.

The people of America were now ready to go to war.

———————

Worldwide Drug Initiative, El Paso, Texas

Slick turned from his computer and stared at Ferrero, the grim expression on his face an indication that something bad had happened. Before he could ask, the computer tech said, "There's been another incident. This time in Arizona."

"Where?"

"Phoenix. Some kind of swingers' establishment. It kicked off three hours ago. Multiple dead and sick. Looks like our man has struck again."

Ferrero cursed and looked down at his watch. It was eleven in the evening. He had a team on the ground in Colombia, and now this. He had hoped that they might get a lead on the killer. Scratching his head, he scanned the ops room. His eyes settled on Teller, who was at his terminal, watching the ISR feed from over Colombia and looking for anything out of the ordinary. "Pete, get Traynor for me."

The master sergeant looked up. "Right away."

"Slick, I need you to find out whatever there is to know about what went on. We need to nail that son of a bitch to the wall."

"I'll get on it."

"Where's Kane?"

"If what we figured is right, they should intercept Blackbird soon."

"All right, keep me posted."

A couple of minutes later, a bleary-eyed Traynor entered the room. "What is it, Luis?"

Ferrero filled him in on what he'd learned and said, "You're going to Phoenix. Take Reynolds with you. If the guy is still on the ground, find him, and get whatever he knows out of him."

"Yes, sir."

"Luis, I have the feed from the swingers' club."

"Send it to me, Slick. I'll look through it too. The more eyes on this, the better."

The operations leader walked over to a desk and sat down at the computer. He opened the file that Swift had sent him and started going through it. It was like watching a B-grade group-sex movie. Then he saw the man with the briefcase.

Ferrero leaned forward in his seat. When there was a group of people around the open briefcase, the man backed up and silently slipped away.

"Once they were hooked, he just left," Ferrero, incredulous at the cold-blooded act, called to Swift. "See if you can track where he went."

The operations manager's eyes remained fixed on his screen, noting that around five minutes elapsed between the supplier's furtive exit and the first person going down. The woman shook violently as a seizure wracked her body. Before long, others joined the macabre dance on the floor. It was disturbing to watch.

Ferrero called to the redheaded computer tech, "What have you got?"

"He got into a vehicle and disappeared."

"Did you get a good shot of his face?"

"Did I what? It's like he smiled for the birdie."

"Good man. Now find out who he is and everything there is to know about him. We'll nail that son of a bitch yet."

Colombia

They took a few steps through the stygian darkness before stopping. A few more, then they paused once more to listen. It was like the old days of the SOG warriors in Vietnam, who stealthily traversed the guerilla-riddled jungle, traveling no more than three hundred meters in a day.

Kane stopped once more and then broke squelch twice. His team acknowledged by repeating the action once. He listened for a moment more before whispering into his comms, "Blackbird, this is Reaper One, copy?"

There was silence, and Kane tried again. "Blackbird, this is Reaper One, copy?"

"Copy, Reaper One." The voice was faint as it came over the comms.

"Roger that, Blackbird. We're here to take you home. We need a location, over."

Newman gave Kane his coordinates, and he checked out the location. "Listen up, Blackbird. We're about one klick west of your position. Sit tight and we'll come for you."

"Copy, Reaper One. Blackbird, out"

"Reaper One, out."

Kane lowered his NVGs and scanned the jungle around him before coming to his feet. Under his body armor, his skin was damp. The 416 in his hands followed his gaze as he did another sweep. "All call signs move out."

The team continued through the jungle on a steady bearing for the next three hours, slow and cautious until Kane stopped them once more and said into his comms, "All call signs hold up. Break. Blackbird, copy?"

"Copy, Reaper One."

"I need a signal. According to our calculations, we should be right on top of you."

"Roger that."

A light flashed in front of them, and Kane said, "Got you. Come ahead."

Newman materialized out of the darkness, his tired gait obvious.

"Blackbird?"

"That's me," Newman confirmed. He took Kane's offered hand. "I'm glad to see you."

"What happened?"

"They hit us out of nowhere. Killed everyone

except me. I managed to get out. I've been on the run ever since. I only managed to lose them an hour or so before you radioed."

"Who were they?" Kane asked. "Militia? Cartel soldiers?"

"Americans."

Kane said nothing, his mind whirling. It made sense. If this was indeed the Cabal, they would be using American ex-military muscle. Newman asked, "What are your orders?"

"Go to Bogota and lay up until we get further instructions."

"But you aren't going to do that, are you?"

"No. We're going back. I want to see what the hell is going on."

"All right. I'm in."

Kane said into his comms, "All call signs on me."

Everyone gathered and waited for Kane to tell them what they already knew. "We're going off-book. Anyone not happy about it, speak now."

No one did.

"Right. Knocker, you're on point. Brick, rear security. Cara, keep an eye on Knocker. Keep your intervals, but for fuck's sake, don't lose touch with the person in front of you. The last thing we need is to be stumbling around, trying to find each other in hostile territory."

He knew he didn't have to say it, but it made him feel better. "OK. Move out."

CHAPTER 11

Washington, DC

The four men weren't happy. After express orders to shut down the operation, another attack had taken place. They discussed how to resolve the situation. Should they bring forward the cleaning process and get rid of Spalding right away, or—

"Send a team to find Orpheus and eliminate him," the first man said. "We need him in the ground before he is found by the local law."

"He is a good operator," the second man said. "He follows orders. Remember that."

"Do you think he's following orders now?" the first man asked.

The second man nodded. "He could be."

"Who is giving them to him?"

"Do you need to ask that question?" the third man asked.

"Spalding?"

"Seems logical, doesn't it? The man is still stricken with grief over the death of his son. He even started the operation without the consent of the Cabal."

"I refuse to believe it without hard evidence," the first man replied.

"Then we need to find Orpheus and ask him."

"Yes. Deploy our Phoenix team."

"What about the operation in Colombia?"

"Destroy it."

"You're not going to wait for Spalding?"

"No. Do we have an asset to do the job?"

The third man nodded. "It can be arranged."

"What about the Bogota team?"

"I will have Rosalie and Darius take care of them."

Colombia

Morning in the jungle dawned hot, humid, and full of bugs. The night had been the same, and Rosalie cursed the disease-infested place silently as she sat up on the thin mattress that had been placed on the wood floor.

She searched around to find what had happened to the black t-shirt she'd been wearing before Darius had ripped it off her and tossed it aside. She rubbed her eyes to clear the sleep away, then tried to find it again. Behind her, Darius groaned and opened his eyes. "What are you doing?" he asked sleepily.

"Trying to find my fucking clothes," she growled.

"Uh-huh." He grunted and closed his eyes once more.

The satellite phone chirped and Rosalie scrambled to her feet, her nakedness on display. As she moved to her pack, the defined muscles on her lithe torso rippled elegantly. She picked the offending communications device up and abruptly answered, "Yes?"

"I trust I didn't wake you, my dear?"

Her demeanor softened. "No, I was already awake."

"I have a job for you and Darius."

"Yes."

"I need you to go to Bogota and take care of the team we have in place there."

"Today?"

"Yes. The sooner, the better."

"All right, I will see to it."

"Before I go," the caller said suddenly, "has your father given you instructions to shut down the operation there?"

"Not yet."

"Hmm. I'm sure he has been busy with our plans this end. Once you have finished in Bogota, you and Darius will return home on a flight being organized for you."

Rosalie hesitated and then asked, "What about the men I brought with me?"

"Their services are no longer required," was the curt reply.

"But they are my men," she protested hotly. Behind her, Darius rose onto an elbow, looking at her askance.

"I appreciate that, Rosalie, but they know too much. They must be sacrificed for the greater good of our country. I'm sorry. Can I trust you to do as I ask?"

"Yes, Uncle."

"Good. Come and see me when you get back."

The call disconnected, and Rosalie turned to Darius. "Get up. We're leaving."

"What's going on?" he asked.

"I'll tell you later."

Cara lowered her binoculars and passed them to Knocker, who lay beside her. She said, "What now, Ike?"

"If you're referring to me as Eisenhower, don't," Kane replied. "He was a lot more structured than me."

"Will you guys work out what we're going to do?" Axe hissed urgently. "I swear I just saw a fucking snake as long as—"

"If you say your dick," Cara said abruptly, "I'm going to come over there and cut it off."

"No, ma'am. It was bigger than that."

The team had spent the morning traversing the jungle, taking their time and exercising all caution. A little before noon, they had slipped into a place where they could observe the camp before them. What they were seeing, however, was disturbing, to say the least.

"They're all Caucasian." Knocker scoffed. "Fucking tossers."

Kane put it out there. "The question is, who do they belong to? Cara, send the feed to HQ. Meanwhile, I'll work out a plan of attack."

"Let's just storm the place, grab them by their meat and two veg, and cut the fuckers off," the SAS man offered."

"What?" Axe asked.

"Just think about what a lot of your girlfriends want to do to you, Axe, and you'll get the drift."

"Oh," he said, and after it sank in, "Ooh."

"This is only a look-see, remember. We get the intel and then get out. We'll wait for dark, then Knocker and I'll go in to see what we can find. After that, we get out and head for Bogota."

"What about my team?" Newman asked.

"I'm sorry. We'll let the right people know their position and leave it to them. At the moment, we've got a war to stop."

Newman nodded. "OK."

They settled in for the afternoon ahead, Axe and Brick taking first watch while the others got some rest. They were an hour in when Swift's voice came over the comms and woke Kane up.

"What is it?"

"I'm picking up an unidentified blip coming in from the east. I'm not sure what it is, but it appears to be some kind of aircraft."

Kane sat up and listened, trying to hear it. "Can you ID it?"

"I can try."

"How far out?"

"Five mikes."

"Could it be a commercial aircraft, Bravo Four?"

"Unlikely."

"If it's not commercial, that leaves military or something else."

"Roger that," Swift said. "However, there are no military airfields in your vicinity, nor are there any to the east."

"Shit," Kane growled. "Bravo Four, I need you to ID that plane *now*."

"I'll do my best."

"Everybody up," Kane said in a low voice.

"What's going on, Reaper?" Knocker asked.

"We've got unidentified inbound air."

They all came erect and began preparing to move when Swift came back on the line. "Reaper, I'm sorry. I fucked up. The signal was screwed. There are two, I repeat, two aircraft. I'm getting a signature comparable to that of a B-One B Lancer. I say again, Reaper, they are a flight of two Bones. Get out. Get out now!"

"Move! Move!" Kane barked at his team. "We've got an airstrike inbound."

The team started to run through the jungle and had gone no more than twenty meters before the first explosion rocked the green canopy.

Twenty-four MK-84 general-purpose bombs rained down from each Lancer. The jungle was torn apart by rapid explosions that unleashed the fires of hell across the landscape.

Kane urged his people on, but the explosions seemed to be chasing them. As they ran through the long grass, the ground dropped sharply away. Without hesitating, they all jumped over the edge and into the abyss.

Phoenix, Arizona

The lead DEA agent eyed the pair suspiciously. "Why wasn't I told you were coming?"

Traynor shrugged. "Maybe someone fucked up."

Randall still wasn't convinced. "I don't know. I need confirmation from Washington before I share anything with you."

"We don't have time for this," Reynolds said, joining the dead-end conversation.

"I can't help that," Randall replied.

After Traynor and Reynolds touched down, they had taken a Tahoe that had been left for them at the airfield outside the city and driven to the DEA Building in central Phoenix. Now they were arguing with the lead agent in charge, demanding to see all the intel amassed so they could analyze it. Traynor was getting pissed about being jerked around, and Reynolds could tell he was about to explode. She looked around the room and saw at least three other agents staring at them. She said, "Do you have an office we can use?"

"Why?"

"Just so we can talk a little more privately," Reynolds said softly, so as not to sound too aggressive. "Please?"

"All right, follow me."

He led them to a separate office and closed the door. "What is it you want?"

Reynolds looked questioningly at Traynor, who gave her a "Be my guest" look. "Agent Randall, as you know, we're from the Worldwide Drug Initiative. We specialize in taking out drug cartels, human traffickers, and arms dealers. Shit, we do just about anything that's asked of us. Right now, we've been asked by Washington to do all we can to stop these mass killings, and we need a little help from you. Sure, you could look elsewhere for permission, but that will waste time. See, we have a window that is rapidly closing, and if we don't achieve what we were sent here to do, more will die."

Randall thought for a moment before he nodded. "All right. What do you need?"

———————

Colombia

Kane coughed and rolled onto his side. The blackness started to fade, and in the distance, he could hear a voice. "Reaper? Talk to me, Reaper. Come on, wake up! That's it."

He opened his eyes, and Brick's face swam in front of him. "Fuck. That was intense."

"Yeah, not wrong. Let's sit you up."

Kane groaned as pain shot through his back. "That hurt. How're the others?"

"We're just fucking dandy," Knocker answered. "We were all knocked ass over tits, but we're operational."

"Uh-huh."

"The cliff blocked most of the blast wave," Cara explained. "You must've hit your head on something when you landed."

"Have you checked in with Bravo?"

Cara nodded. "Yes."

"I'd like to know why an airstrike was brought in using Lancers," Axe growled.

Cara said, "The general is looking into it, but I think we can assume what their aim was."

"Sterilize the factory," Kane said.

"That would be my guess."

"Help me up, Brick," the Team Reaper commander requested.

"What are you doing?" he asked, pushing down on Kane's shoulder so he couldn't rise.

"We need to get back in there and look it over. See if we can come up with something that'll help us out before the Colombian government gets troops into the area."

Brick nodded and helped him to his feet. Kane took a little time to gather himself before taking his first step. That done, he took a second, then another. "All good. Let's go."

"What if we find survivors?" Newman asked.

"Nothing could survive that. The drop was designed that way."

They climbed the rugged cliff and took in the scene before them, which was akin to an apocalyptic movie. Trees were shredded and blown apart. The earth was black where it had been scorched, and the sun shone on the ground for the first time in eons since the canopy was no longer there. Debris from the factory was strewn in all directions as though a giant had thrown a tantrum and flung it far and wide. Fires still burned, and smoke filled the air with a strong smell.

As Kane had said, there was nothing left. It was all gone. Almost…

"Over here," Knocker called. "Brick, over here."

The team medic hurried over to where the SAS man was crouched beside the half-blackened figure of what used to be a man. Kane joined them, and when he looked down, he could see the charred, blistered skin on half of the man's body. Something had shielded the other half. Then there was the leg, or what was left of it—a bloody stump ending just above the knee, with a pinky-white bone protruding from the mutilated appendage.

"H-help m-me," he stammered.

Kane heard Brick say as he opened his Unit One pack and took out some morphine, "What's your name, buddy?"

"W-Will."

"Hey, Will. My name's Brick. I'm going to be your medic today. We'll give you something for the pain and see about getting you out of here. OK?"

The man named Will gave him a slight nod. "Who-who are y-you?"

"We're the people who're going to get you out once you're stabilized," Brick lied. He went after more morphine. "My commanding officer will call in a medevac, and you'll be out of here in no time. "What were you doing down here?"

"Working for Bright Spark Solutions."

"Doing what, *compadre?*" Brick asked.

The dying man gave a macabre grin. "M-making d-drugs."

Kane stood quietly and listened to every word that the man said. He leaned close to Brick and whispered, "Ask him who was in charge."

"Will, who was in charge of the operation?"

The dying man took his time answering. Waves of pain were flowing though his body despite the morphine, and shock was setting in. Then he managed, "Rosie and Darius."

"Rosie? Who is Rosie?"

"Rosalie Spalding."

"Rest easy, Will. I'll give you a bit more morphine and you'll go to sleep. When you wake up, you'll be good to go."

Kane watched Brick work, then the medic climbed to his feet. He turned to Kane, who asked, "How are we meant to get him out?"

"We don't. I just gave him enough morphine to stop a horse. He was going to die anyway. I just helped it along. There was nothing I could do. The poor bastard was in a lot of pain."

Kane nodded his understanding. He pressed the transmit button on his comms and said, "Bravo, copy?"

"Zero here, Reaper One. Read you Lima Charlie. How is everyone?"

"Team is all fine. They cleaned house. We've just managed to get some intel you might be interested in. Three names. Bright Spark Solutions, Darius, and Rosalie Spalding. The latter were here in Colombia, running this side of the operation. Their current status is unknown."

"Was that 'Spalding,' Reaper One?"

"Affirmative."

"Roger that."

"We're going to move out to Bogota, Zero."

"Copy. Keep us posted."

"Roger. Reaper One out."

Kane gathered the others around him. "All right, it's time we got out of here. Move out."

CHAPTER 12

Worldwide Drug Initiative, El Paso, Texas

"OK, listen up. We've got some names. Teller, I want you to monitor the team channel, and Slick, you run down these names. Get to it."

Ferrero had just finished speaking when Thurston appeared. "What's happening?"

"I've got some names: Bright Spark Solutions, Darius, and Rosalie Spalding. Reaper told me the latter were running the Bogota end of the operation."

"Rosalie Spalding? That sounds like the lead we've been waiting for."

"It does. I've got Slick running them down. It shouldn't take long."

Thurston walked to Swift's computer terminal. The redheaded tech looked up at her and smiled. "It be a cinch on two at least, ma'am."

A couple of moments later, he brought up information on the first name. "Bright Spark Solutions, ma'am. Run by a man named Clive Rogers. Ex-Marine from back in the day."

A picture of a thickset man with dark hair and a chest full of ribbons appeared.

"He has changed a bit, though." He put up a different picture. This one had Rogers with gray hair and a lined face. "He's in his early sixties now."

"What sort of services does Bright Spark provide?"

"You name it—security, kidnap extract; they've even been suspected of helping out the odd coup. They're a full-on military contractor, ma'am. They're like an army for a small country."

"Talk to me about Rosalie Spalding."

Swift punched in a few keys, and her picture swapped with that of Rogers. She too wore a uniform. "Rosalie Spalding served in the military, as you can see. Rose to the rank of lieutenant colonel before she got out with full honors."

"What else?"

"As you've already guessed, her father is Senator Marc Spalding—" He stopped. Frowned.

"What is it?"

"Rosalie Spalding and Rogers are related."

"How so?" Thurston asked.

"He's her uncle. Mother's brother."

Thurston nodded. "What does the mother do?'

"Nothing. She died five years back."

"How?"

"Car accident."

Thurston stopped and thought. "Anything on Darius?"

"No, ma'am."

"OK. Keep at it."

The general walked to one side and took out her cell. She punched in a number, which was picked up by Melissa Smith. "You have news?"

"Is this call being recorded?"

"Yes."

"Don't."

A couple of moments later, Smith said, "Go."

"What do you know about Bright Spark Solutions and Rosalie Spalding?"

"You got something, Mary?" Melissa asked.

"Someone hit the Ranger team in Colombia," Thurston explained. "They took seventy-five percent casualties, and I had to send Reaper in with his team to extract a survivor. Then, not long ago, someone tried to blow the shit out of them with B1 Lancers."

"Are they OK?"

"Affirmative. Someone cleaned house down there, but Kane managed to get some intel. Bright Spark Solutions and Rosalie Spalding. I've had my guy running them down, and he tells me that the man who owns Bright Spark is Rosalie Spalding's uncle."

"Shit. Bright Spark is the biggest private military contractor in the US. The CIA has been keeping an eye on them secretly, but we haven't come up with a lot. We think they were responsible for a coup in Central Africa last year. We tried to get someone on the inside, but it failed abysmally."

"Do you think that they...I mean, Rogers, is part of the Cabal?"

"It's possible, I suppose. His private army is certainly big enough. He'd need a lot more than that, though."

"But it would be a big part of it?"

"Yes."

"It's a place to start. I'm hoping we can pick up Rosalie Spalding and the supplier sooner rather than later."

"Be careful, Mary. Those people are powerful."

"I'm beginning to understand that."

Thurston hung up and went over to Ferrero. "Melissa?"

"Yes. She said they've been watching Bright Spark for a while."

A noise from the workstations made them turn. Swift was hurrying toward them, a look of excitement on his face. "I think I've found him."

"Who?" Ferrero asked.

"The supplier. He popped up on a street cam in Phoenix."

"Let Traynor and Reynolds know. I hope he'll be in custody by the end of the day."

———

Phoenix, Arizona

Traynor eased the top half of his body around the corner of the building and stared at the one opposite, where the target was said to have taken refuge. He pulled his head back and shook it. "Is Slick sure that this is where he is?"

"The camera doesn't lie," Reynolds replied.

"Shit." He looked around the corner once more. "We should have brought backup."

Reynolds smiled at him. "You have me."

"I'll try to remember that when we're getting reamed by those assholes," Traynor told her gruffly.

"How do you want to do this?"

"We'll just walk in the front door and see what happens."

"I like it," Reynolds said. "Nice and simple."

"Let's go. Stay close and watch your six."

They cleared the building and walked across the street toward a rundown bar with twenty or so motorcycles sitting out front. The sign above the awning read *Snake Den*, which filled him with confidence.

When they pushed in through the door, the warmth of the fetid interior air hit them in the face as it rushed to escape. Even their stink didn't want to hang out with the outlaw bikers.

Describing the interior as dim would be a gross understatement. Traynor thought NVGs might have been beneficial for the task at hand, but since he'd forgotten to pack them, it was what it was. A large stage took up the bulk of the real estate in the center of the room, with a chrome pole running from the stained wooden planks toward the ceiling. There, making virtual love to it, was a scantily clad young lady with large breasts and long blonde hair.

Catcalls and whistles emanated from various types seated around the bar. A large biker with a bushy beard leaned in and slipped a bill into her G-string. Then he tried to climb onto the stage with her, bringing on a huge cheer from the already noisy crowd. The young woman straightened up, raised her stilettoed foot, and rammed it into his face, forcing him back. Two burly men with bald heads stepped forward and dragged him away.

"Looks like the animals are in the house tonight," Reynolds said to Traynor.

As they headed for the bar, many of the bikers turned their attention to them. Reynolds said, "I'm going to take two showers tonight."

Traynor ignored her, and when the man behind the bar came over to serve them, he ordered two beers. The thickset barman walked off, then returned with the drinks. Traynor tossed some money on the bar top and said, "We're looking for this man. You seen him?"

He slid a picture forward. The barman didn't look at it before saying, "Nope."

"Take a look."

"I told you, I ain't seen him."

"Listen, this is real—"

"Hey, we got a cop in here," shouted a biker who'd overheard the conversation.

They all froze. The conversations stopped, and the woman ceased gyrating around the pole. A thin hiss of air escaped Traynor's lips. "Shit."

Out of the crowd waded a giant of a man. His body was heavily tattooed, and he sported a thick beard. His nose was crooked from being broken one time too many without being set, and he had a large belly.

"What the fuck are pigs doing in our bar?" he snarled.

"We're looking for someone," Traynor said.

"You are, are you?" The big man sneered. "Not now. You're done. Get out."

"Can't do that," Reynolds said.

Big Man turned his head to look at her. His eyes lit with lust as he said, "Hello, pretty."

"Hey, ugly."

Traynor winced.

The big biker stepped closer to Reynolds, and she could smell the sour odor of his unwashed body. She wrinkled her nose. "You need a bath."

For a big man, his reflexes were lightning-fast. He reached out and got a brutal hold on her left arm. "You need to watch your mouth, bitch," he hissed.

"And you need to back the fuck up, asshole, before I blow your balls off."

The big man's jaw dropped as he let her arm go and

took a step back. He looked down at the M17 in her fist, then gave her a nervous smile. "You're bluffing."

"Try me, asshole," she shot back. "Take a look at my friend's picture. He's wanted for killing a lot of people."

The biker shifted his gaze and stared at the picture of the man the pair wanted. He gave a slight nod and said, "He was here."

"Was?" Traynor asked.

"Is. In the far corner."

Traynor had just turned around to look when the barroom went dark and all hell broke loose.

As soon as the power was cut, the sound of glass shattering filtered through protesting shouts. Then three flashbangs detonated.

Traynor and Reynolds dropped to the floor, their ears ringing from the piercing sound. The bikers staggered and held their heads. The front door burst open and dark figures appeared, filling the void.

Thin shafts of red light from laser sights mounted on top of automatic weapons danced around the room. Sudden gunfire erupted and indiscriminate bullets reached out, punching and tearing into flesh. Cries of pain came from the wounded and dying. Through the ringing in her ears, Reynolds could make out the screams of a woman and had the fleeting thought that it might have been the stripper. She brought her M17 up, looking to bring in into line with a target, but there were too many bodies in motion for her to get a clear shot.

Beside her, Traynor had his weapon out too and was doing the same. A wild storm of lead whipped around their crouching figures, and they both knew it was only a matter of time before one of them went down.

"On me!" Traynor shouted and started to make his way to the left. A biker staggered into him and almost knocked him flat. The man jerked violently as a couple of rounds hammered into him, and he fell next to the ex-DEA man.

Finally, Traynor reached his destination and hunkered down behind the stage. When Reynolds crouched beside him, she saw the stripper lying on her back and muzzle flashes all around.

She set her jaw in anger and looked for a target. Raising her weapon in an outstretched hand, Brooke waited for an opportunity. She fired twice when it appeared and was rewarded by a shadowy figure toppling to the side.

"What the hell are you doing?" Traynor snapped. "You'll kill civilians."

"Well, what the fuck are we supposed to do?" she snarled back in helpless exasperation.

"Wait."

So she waited, and within a couple of heartbeats, the opportunity arose. Traynor said, "Now!"

They rose and took targets of opportunity. The M17s bucked in their hands, and three of the bar attackers fell to the ground. At least five more were still standing. Weapons roared as the attackers emptied their magazines at Reynolds and Traynor, bullets chewing gouges in the wooden stage. Reynolds felt a burn along her cheek as a thin sliver of wood sliced a neat cut in her flesh. Blood trickled immediately, but she ignored it to fire when the bullets stopped. When she looked to aim, there was nothing to shoot at. The attackers were gone.

"Pete?" she said, confused.

"Yeah, I see it."

They both came to their feet and moved toward the door, stepping over bodies. While Traynor went outside, Reynolds checked the shooters. All were beyond help. The ex-DEA agent came back inside and said, "Well?"

"They're all done?"

He nodded. "Check the dead. See if our man is amongst them."

"How? It's too dark."

Traynor went to the nearest fallen biker and patted his body down. He found what he wanted and reached into the dead man's pocket to retrieve a lighter. He flicked it, and the flame came alive. It took a couple of minutes, but they found their man. He'd been shot three times. "I guess we know why they came here," Reynolds said.

"Yes," Traynor replied. "Now we're back to square one."

———

Washington, DC

"The Phoenix team had to kill the asset," Rogers said into the cell. "The Worldwide Drug Initiative had two people on the ground. It was easier to do it that way."

"Those people are becoming a pain in my ass," the voice on the other end said.

"Yes, sir."

"So we have no way of knowing if your dear brother-in-law told him to carry out the extra attack."

"I daresay he did, sir," Rogers admitted. "I have instructed the others that after the vote, he is to be terminated."

"What about his daughter?"

"What about her?"

"Can she be relied on?"

"Yes. I have no reason to doubt her loyalty."

"Do it right away."

"But what about the vote?" Rogers asked.

"It will go ahead whether he is there or not. The man was careless and has become a liability. I want him gone. Once the war starts, we can move in to secure the trizanthium. Once that's done, it can be utilized for the upcoming hostilities that will engulf Europe."

"Yes, sir. There is one more thing. The factory in Colombia was destroyed. However, it would seem that the WDI has a second team on the ground."

"Don't you have a team in Colombia? The ones who assassinated the ambassador?"

"Not for much longer. Loose ends."

"I see. Then you'd better come up with a way to address the problem."

"I'll take care of it."

The line went dead, and Rogers looked at his watch. It was eleven o'clock. He pressed a couple of buttons and waited for Spalding to pick up. "What is it?"

"I need to see you."

"When?"

"Tonight. I'll be there in an hour."

"I'll be expecting you."

Once more the line went dead, and this time, Rogers put the cell in his pocket. After crossing his office, he opened a cupboard that contained a safe and input the combination to unlock it. He removed a handgun and suppressor and put them into his other pocket. Then he left the room, turning out the lights as he went.

———

"What is so important that you needed to see me?" Spalding asked abruptly.

Rogers looked around the lavish library, all the bookcases stacked with first-edition collectibles. "I'm impressed, Marc. All these books you have. I would never have thought to see them all in one place. Apart from a library, that is. Not in a private collection. You must be proud of it."

"Stop dicking around, Clive. You came here for a reason, so spit it out."

Rogers nodded and sat down opposite Spalding on the far side of the oak desk. He sighed. "You're right. I had a call from you-know-who tonight."

"Yes? What did he want?"

"He is displeased that things have gotten out of hand," Rogers told his brother-in-law. He paused, then, "Shit, Marc. What were you thinking, jumping the fucking gun like that?"

"It needed to be done," Spalding snapped.

"When we were ready," Rogers reminded him. "Once American forces were on the ground, I was to put Bright Spark contractors in to secure the mine sites."

"The vote will go ahead, and from the numbers, I've been told it is only a formality. That war will be declared against Colombia."

"And if you'd have waited, you would have been there to see it," Rogers said in a calm voice.

"What are you—" Then it registered why his brother-in-law was there. He nodded. "I see."

"You should have waited, Craig. Fuck, you should have waited."

"Did you volunteer?"

"No. This came from the top, but I'd already decided it would happen anyway," Clive said honestly. You've become too much of a loose cannon, and the

Cabal can't afford people like you."

"Can't you—"

POP, POP

Spalding jerked, and a shocked expression went across his face. He looked down and saw the blood start to spread across his middle. When he looked back up, he saw the suppressed handgun in Rogers' fist. "Sorry, Craig."

Before he left, Rogers threw the weapon on the floor so it could be found by the proper authorities.

CHAPTER 13

Bright Spark Safe House, Bogota, Colombia

The scent of freshly spilled blood hung heavy in the air. The interior of the house looked more like it belonged in Syria than here in Bogota. Bodies were strewn across the floor, and the walls had holes punched in the plaster. Rosalie placed a fresh magazine in her MP5SD and swept the room for any final threats.

To her left, Darius shot a moaning figure who lay prostrate on the floor. The man lurched and went still. "Any more?"

"No, I think that's it."

"Good, then it's time to leave."

The satellite phone on her belt rang, and she answered it. Rosalie listened, looked around the room, and said, "You could have come to me with this twenty minutes ago."

The call disconnected and Darius asked, "What is it?"

"There is a second team. They were picked up by satellite after the factory was taken care of."

"And now they want us to take care of them?"

Rosalie nodded. "We're going to have to use the local authorities."

"They'll have to find them first."

"That's the thing about being one of the most powerful organizations in the world. We already know where they are."

Bogota Colombia

The team had appropriated a truck and used it to travel the five hours to Bogota, where they found the CIA safe house Melissa Smith had offered them the use of. Two officers met them there and allowed them to use their communications equipment so Kane could report in.

The house was old but well kept. From the street, it was unassuming, blending with every other family home on the block, but beneath the surface was a sub-section with all the latest gadgetry the operatives of the CIA required. Including an armory.

"We've reached the nest, Luis," Kane told him. "How're things back home?"

Ferrero told him about the headway they'd made and the episode in Phoenix.

"Is everyone OK?"

"Yes, they're fine."

"How do we proceed from here?" Kane asked.

"Continue your search for Rosalie Spalding and her off-sider. Slick is working on finding out where the ambassador's kill team originated from. Until then, get some rest."

Kane signed off and came back upstairs to find one of the CIA officers talking on a handheld radio. "All right, Eagle One. Bring it in. We'll be waiting for you. Out."

The officer, whose name was Rollings, turned to Kane and said, "Looks like it's the night for it."

"What's up?"

"There is a Delta team on the ground, and they're looking for a place to lay up for the night."

"What's a Delta team doing in-country? We're not at war yet, are we?"

Rollings shook his head. "I've no idea. I guess we'll find out when they arrive. They're about ten mikes out."

The rest of Kane's team was spread out on various pieces of furniture and the floor in the large living room. Axe was snoring softly, lying flat on his back on the floor. Cara was on the only sofa with her eyes closed, but he could tell she was still awake from her breathing. Brick sat in a chair in the corner, reading a book he'd found, while Knocker and Newman were deep in conversation about different locations they'd served in around the world. "What's up, Reaper?" Cara asked without opening her eyes.

"We've got a Delta team coming in to join us. Things are going to be a bit tight for a while."

"Any progress on the hit team?" Brick asked, looking up from his reading.

"Not yet, but it looks like our friends are still cleaning house. They killed their man who was supplying the poisoned drugs. It seems they're determined to leave no loose ends. They took out a bar full of bikers to do it. Those people have no fear."

The Delta team arrived on time, four men led by a sergeant named Tom Coles. Right away, he and Kane got together to compare notes. It seemed the D-Boys were in-country with the same objective as Kane and his team: trying to find whoever was responsible for what happened to the ambassador.

"You find anything?" Kane asked.

Coles nodded. He was a big man with broad shoulders and dark hair. "We found where they were holed up. Only problem was they were all dead. Someone got there before us."

"How long?"

"An hour at most."

"They're still cleaning house," Kane muttered.

Coles frowned. "Who?"

"The ones responsible for this whole mess," Kane told him. "Tell me, were they American?"

"How did you know?"

"Our computer guy managed to get us a line on

something they said that didn't correlate with who they were masquerading as."

Coles stared at Kane for a moment and said, "You know something, Kane. What the fuck is going on?"

"I'll give you the short version because the long one is too complicated. Someone is trying to start a war with Colombia for personal gain. The poisoned drugs were just the start of it. I presume the assassination of the ambassador was to kick it over the edge."

"Holy cow!"

"That's right. A Ranger unit was sent into the jungle to find the factory they were using and were ambushed. Newman out there is the only one left. We extracted him, but before we could get away, someone bombed the shit out of our target to cover everything up."

"You have any idea who?"

Kane shook his head. "Sorry, Coles. We'll have to file that one under need to know. I wish I could tell you more, but at this time, the less you know, the safer you and your team will be."

"Damn it, Kane!"

"Heads up. We've got a problem." Rollings' warning turned their heads, and they saw the troubled expression on his face.

"What is it?"

"Colombian military closing on our position."

"WTF?" Kane growled. He came to his feet, followed by Coles.

They hurried to where their teams were relaxing and Kane snapped, "Everybody up. Time to go to work. We've got Colombian military inbound."

"ROEs, Reaper?" Axe asked.

"Hold your fire until told otherwise, Axe."

Coles said, "My men will take the rear of the house. Keep your eyes open for creepers."

"Axe, Cara, take the front," Kane added. "Knocker and Brick, take the sides. Call them as you see them. Let's kill the lights and get our NVGs on. Looks like we're going to war."

"This is bollocks, this is," Knocker growled. "We finally find a nice place to rest in a tropical country, and someone comes along and fucks it up. I've a good mind to stick my head out there and tell them to sod off."

Coles gave Kane a confused look.

"Take no notice of him. He's British."

"And they fucking can't speak English," Axe added.

Cara smiled at the Delta man as she walked past him, shrugging into her body armor. "It's complicated."

Kane and Coles hurried downstairs to the communications room to view the security feed. Four screens covered each side of the house and its approaches. "What have we got?" Reaper One asked.

"There are three trucks coming in. I'd estimate thirty men."

They watched the vehicles pull up and disgorge their human cargo. Rollings said, "They're Urban Counter-Terrorism Special Forces Group. AFEUR, for the uneducated."

"I've dealt with them before," Kane said. "Not people you want to tangle with. They'll hit us hard."

"Then we'll have to hit them back harder," Coles replied. He turned away and went back upstairs.

"How did they know about this place?" Kane asked Rollings.

"Your guess is as good as mine."

As he watched, Kane's mind ticked over until he finally said out loud, "They know we're here."

"Who?"

"The people responsible for the ambassador. The military is here for us. They told them where we are. Can you hook into our comms?"

"Yes."

"Good. Keep an eye out for anything hinky."

Kane took the steps two at a time and made his way to the front of the house. He was in the living room with Cara, who'd pushed the sofa against the window. Once the shooting started, it would be the only protection she would have. She'd already broken the window so it wouldn't implode and shower her with dangerous shards of glass. Her NVGs were down and her 416 was up. "You got anything yet?"

"Not since I saw lights out beyond the perimeter," she informed him.

"Don't worry. They'll be here directly."

"Bring it on."

He patted her on the shoulder. "Oorah."

From there, he ducked in to check on Axe. The big man was hunkered down behind his M249 SAW. Like Cara, he had broken the window to avoid any danger from it during the coming firefight. "How you doing, Marine?"

"We're all just fine and dandy, Reaper," he replied. "Just wish they'd hurry up and get it on."

"How you set for ammo?"

"All good."

"Keep your head down."

"Can't shoot them if you can't see them," Axe shot back.

"Can't see them if you haven't got a head," Kane told him. "Keep it down."

They were twelve against thirty. Three to one odds—not the best, but not the worst. The defenders waited in silence for what would ensue.

"In the house!"

It was a woman's voice.

"Can you hear me?"

Kane hurried to the living room and crouched near Cara. "This is an unexpected turn."

"Who do you figure she is?" Cara asked. "She sounds American."

"If I had to hazard a guess, I would say it's Rosalie Spalding."

"I know you're in there, men of the CIA."

"I suppose we'd better ask what she wants," Kane sighed. "Keep an eye out for creepers. You see anything, put them down."

"Roger that," Cara said, not turning away.

"We hear you!" Kane called back.

"Good. We want the American mercenary team you have. They are wanted for the deaths of some civilians—"

Kane cut her off. "What mercenaries?"

"I know they are there. Don't make us come for them. It wouldn't go easy for you. Send them out, and that is where it will end."

"Somehow I don't believe her," Cara muttered.

"I guess you know that if you come in here after them, a lot of people will die."

Brick's voice came through the comms. "Reaper, we've got movement around this side."

"The bastards are over here too," Knocker informed him.

Coles' voice made the verdict unanimous. They were surrounded.

"I will give you two minutes to think about it. After that, you will all die."

Kane pressed his comms button and said, "Keep an eye out. They'll be coming in a moment."

Suddenly the SAW from the other room erupted, and bullets streaked across the yard. Cries of alarm echoed throughout the staccato hammering, and Axe's voice came over the comms feed. "Contact front!"

All at once, the whole house lit up as bullets ripped into it from every direction. Drywall and debris started to rain down inside as slugs shredded the interior walls into confetti. Kane brought his 416 up and found a target kneeling near a small bush. He hit him with two shots before returning to his low crouch.

Beside him, he could hear Cara methodically firing as she picked her targets. That was the sniper in her.

From the rear of the house, Kane could hear the Delta boys' weapons rattling as they cut down the attackers who thought their presence was unknown. The Colombians were realizing they'd underestimated the force within the safehouse.

As another storm of lead whipped through the glassless window, Kane said into his comms, "Reaper Five and Three, how're we all looking?"

"Five is OK."

"Blimey, those wankers are getting their ambitions mixed up with their capabilities, Reaper. I just had one tosser walk up to the window like he was on a night out. Dickhead."

Kane grinned and said, "I take it you're fine, Reaper Three?"

"Just brilliant, Reaper. Just brilliant."

Kane rose again and fired at a figure as it dove behind a bush. He waited to see if it would reemerge, and when it did, the shooter had crawled slightly to his left. Kane shifted his aim, but the shooter was already firing, and Kane's aim was thrown off as he squeezed the trigger. "Damn it!"

"Looks like you could do with some time on the

range," Cara called.

"Shut up and keep shooting."

She chuckled and fired twice more, then dropped out her spent magazine before reloading a fresh one.

In a sudden blaze of light, the outside of the house lit up as outgoing tracer rounds streaked across the yard from Axe's SAW. What sounded like "Yahoo!" came from the other room. Kane guessed the big ex-Recon Marine was enjoying the light show.

Once more, Kane went to his comms. "Delta One, copy?"

"Read you Lima Charlie, Reaper One."

"How you guys doing out there?"

"All OK."

"Roger that." He turned to Cara. "You right here for a minute?"

"I'm—fuck, RPG!"

The rocket-propelled grenade fizzed across the yard and slammed into the house between the two front rooms. The building shook violently as part of the structure collapsed from the blast. Kane felt a heatwave wash over him, and the ceiling came down right before everything went black.

Worldwide Drug Initiative, El Paso, Texas

"What happened?" Thurston snapped as she stormed

into the operations room.

"We lost contact with the team," Ferrero told her. "One moment they were there, and then they were gone. All we know is that they were in heavy contact and then nothing."

"In heavy contact with who?" the general asked.

"Colombian Special Forces," he explained.

"What? How the hell did that happen?"

"Unsure at this time, but you can bet that the Cabal is behind it somewhere. That's not all. They're holed up with a Delta team. It seems they were down there looking for the same team we were."

"A Delta team? Who sent them?"

"No idea. But they found them, and every last one of them was dead. The cleaners were there before them. You can guess who did the job."

"Rosalie Spalding and Darius."

"If I was of a mind, I'd be shouting bingo about now."

"Do we have a bird overhead?"

"Slick is trying to find one as we speak."

"Slick has found one," the computer tech interrupted.

They hurried to his station and looked down at his screen. Whatever was coming was taking its time loading, and Thurston said, "Big screen."

A couple of keystrokes later, the ISR feed appeared. "Where are we getting this?"

"The NSA was kind enough to let me use it without their knowledge. There are a shitload of satellites up there we can choose from, and they all seem to be gathering intel on Colombia. My guess is someone is making plans for war. Except—"

"Except what?"

"There's one that doesn't belong to anyone I've ever heard of."

"A private one?" Thurston asked doubtfully. "That's almost unheard of."

"But it's there."

"Have a look at it," she ordered as she watched the screen.

The battle raged on at the rear of the house, but it looked as though the front had collapsed. "Good grief," Thurston hissed. "Where's the nearest help?"

Ferrero shook his head. "The closest is a carrier task group in the Pacific."

"Damn it. Keep trying to raise them. They need to get out of there *now*."

———————

CIA Safehouse, Bogota Colombia

Kane hurt. He wasn't sure what part it was as he came out of the darkness, but it sure as shit pained him. He moaned and tried to move.

"Take it easy, Reaper," a voice said.

"What happened?"

"The roof came down."

His eyes snapped open. "Cara!"

"I'm here."

He sat up and turned to face the voice. He could see Brick working by flashlight on her leg. "What happened to you?"

"It's just a scratch. Brick is stitching it up."

Kane climbed to his feet and wobbled, then gathered himself. "Where's my ballistic helmet?"

Brick tossed it to him. Kane put it on and then realized something. No one was shooting. "What's going on. It's quiet."

"We're all taking a breather. Getting ready for the next dance."

"I wish," the Team Reaper commander said. "They're regrouping."

"Without a doubt."

"Are we the only casualties from the RPG?"

"Yeah," Brick said. "Good thing you all ducked."

"What about Axe?"

"You know him. Head like rock."

Kane nodded. He reached up and pressed his transmit button. "Zero, copy?"

"Waste of time," Cara said. "We're all dark."

"Shit. All right, hang tight. I'll be back in a moment."

Kane struggled through the debris, making his way downstairs to check in with Rollings. He was relieved to see that some of the security cameras were still operational. "How's it looking out there?"

"It's reasonably quiet at the moment. For how

long, who knows?"

"You spooks have another way out of here?"

He gave Kane a wry smile. "The back door?"

Kane nodded. "Nothing like a sense of humor when you're neck-deep in shit. I'll go check on the others."

He went back upstairs and to the rear of the house, where he found Coles. "I see you're back on your feet."

"Hard head," Kane replied. "What's happening out here?"

"Quiet," Coles replied. "Too quiet if you ask me."

"We have to work out a way to get clear."

"There's only one way I can see."

"I think I know what it is."

"Shoot our way out."

Kane made a clicking sound with his tongue. "That's it. What do you have that goes bang?"

"Some grenades—flashbangs."

"Let's get everyone ready. We're getting out of here."

Kane returned to where Brick was finishing up with Cara. "Are you done, Brick?"

"Yes, she's good to rejoin the fight."

"Do you think you can walk on it? Maybe run?" he asked Cara.

"Just try to stop me."

"Good. We're getting out. Brick, fetch Axe and Knocker. Cara and I will head out the back to the D-boys."

"Don't forget the spooks," the ex-SEAL reminded

him.

"I suppose I'd better tell Rollings what's going on."

He went back down to the communications room and found the CIA officer where he'd left him, although this time, he was trying to get communications back up. He looked at Kane. "It's fucked."

"Don't worry about it. We're getting out. Do you have measures in place to deal with it?"

Rollings nodded. "Once they kick off, we'll have two minutes to get clear of the place before it blows."

"Hopefully it'll be enough. Start the countdown."

Kane joined Coles, who was still at his post with his men. Kane said, "You want to lead out, or you want us to?"

Coles looked at him and said, "Two of my men will lead. You put your banged-up soldier in the center so we can keep an eye on her. Have one of yours pull rear security."

"Don't let Cara hear you say that. She'll have you for breakfast."

"I have no doubt," Coles agreed.

Rollings joined them. "We've got about a minute and a half."

Coles frowned. "For what?"

"Until this place goes boom."

"Shit. Let's move."

They blew out the back of the safe house with the utmost ease. The Colombian special forces, not expecting there to be so many operators, were taken by surprise. Coles' D-boys carved through the perimeter, and the rest of the group followed them into the night. When the timer ran out, the strategically placed charges tore through what remained of the safe house, obliterating any evidence of the building's real purpose. The explosion rocked the surrounding homes, set off car alarms, and dogs started howling. Watching from nearby, the orange glow lighting her face, was Rosalie Spalding.

CHAPTER 14

Worldwide Drug Initiative HQ, El Paso, Texas

The tension in the operations center eased slightly once they found out that all team members were alive. Traynor and Reynolds had made it back to El Paso safely and were a few minutes out. Teller was watching the ISR feed over Bogota, relieved that Kane and both teams were moving to an extract. Slick was still running down leads on Bright Spark, and Ferrero was sitting in a chair, feet up, eyes closed, playing Beethoven's Fifth inside his head. Meanwhile, Thurston had placed a call to Melissa Smith to give her an update, and she was now speaking to Hank Jones.

"That's about it, sir. Things have been pretty fluid here."

"It would seem so, Mary. I'll update the President in person. Do you have much on Rogers?"

"No, sir. We have almost nothing. The Cabal continues to clean up after themselves. They leave nothing for us. We really need to find Rosalie Spalding so we can bring her in, but it's too hot in Colombia. It appears that certain elements in their Armed Forces have been paid off. Maybe we can dig up something on Senator Spalding."

"I'm afraid that's a dead end too, Mary," Jones said. "And I do mean dead."

"What? When?"

"Last night. Someone shot him."

"For fuck's sake," she hissed in a low voice.

"What was that?"

"Nothing, sir."

"I'm sorry, Mary. You'll have to find something else."

Thurston sighed. "I suppose there is one positive thing, sir. The poisoned drugs are off the street, and the man who distributed them is no more."

"That is one way to look at it," Jones agreed.

"Damn it, Hank," she exploded. "Those fucking assholes pissed me off. They've gone after my team on numerous occasions, and it's going to stop."

"What do you propose, Mary?"

"Once the team is back together, I want to start taking them off the board."

"Careful, Mary. You're starting to sound like the commander of a CIA wet team."

"You're right, but what other way is there to do it?"

"I'm sure you'll find a way. I'll talk to you tomorrow. Oh, by the way, the vote has been brought forward to today. If it goes the way it's expected to, United States military forces will be moving into forward staging areas by tonight."

"When will they jump off?"

"Sooner rather than later."

"I'll brief you if anything comes up, General."

"Take care, Mary."

She disconnected the call and got up from her seat, then went into the operations room and saw Ferrero laid back in a chair. Before she could say anything, he murmured, "I'm not asleep. I'm just figuring out how to do it is all."

Thurston smiled. "When you work out the secret, let me know."

He opened his eyes and put his feet on the floor. "I'm so not a young man anymore."

"Me neither. I want to curl up with a nice warm man and close my eyes."

Ferrero stared at her.

"Damn it!" she exclaimed. "Did I say that out loud?"

"I'll pretend I didn't hear it."

"Something I did just hear," she said to him. "The general told me Marc Spalding is dead."

"Really?" There was surprise in Ferrero's voice.

Thurston nodded. "Someone shot him."

"Those people sure are serious about tying up their loose ends."

"Excuse me, ma'am," Teller said, interrupting

their conversation. "Looks like we have visitors."

They turned to look at him and the master sergeant nodded at the smaller security screen. Two black SUVs had pulled up in the lot and four men were climbing out of them. "Everything about them says law enforcement of some kind," the general noted.

"They have that certain something about them," Ferrero agreed.

"Teller, go and meet them at the door," Thurston ordered.

A few minutes later, the four men were inside the WDI HQ and introduced themselves as FBI. The agent in charge went by the name of Walls. "Ma'am," he said. "I...we're sorry to impose upon you this way, but you need to come with us to Washington."

She looked at him incredulously. "I what?"

"We need to escort you to El Paso International Airport, where a plane is waiting to fly you to Washington."

"The hell you will," Thurston snapped. "I'm overseeing an operation at this time. It'll have to wait."

"I'm sorry, ma'am, but it can't. I'm under strict instructions to take you in."

"Whoa," Ferrero said, taking a step forward. "What's 'this take you in' bullshit?"

"Back off, sir," Walls' voice took on a strict official tone. "If you come any closer, I'll have my men arrest you."

"What's going on?" Traynor asked as he and

Reynolds walked through the door.

"Just remain where you are, sir," Walls snapped. The strain in his voice caused his men to drop their hands to their weapons.

"Whoa, what the fuck?" Traynor said and drew his weapon.

In a second, the situation went from relative calm to sitting on a knife-edge. Thurston knew if she didn't regain control, things could spiral quickly.

"Stand down!" she snarled. "Do it now! Traynor, put your gun away. Agent Walls, tell your men to take their hands away from their guns."

Traynor lowered his weapon and holstered it. Walls looked at his men, who moved their hands away from their weapons. That seemed to defuse the immediate risk of gunplay, although tension was still heightened in the room.

"Now," Thurston started once more, "tell me why I need to go to Washington?"

"You're needed to answer questions regarding the murder of Senator Marc Spalding."

"Why?"

"You just are."

"You'll have to do better than that," Thurston told him.

"A gun registered to you was found at the scene of the crime."

The general chuckled. "Is this some kind of fucking joke? If it is, I don't have any time for it, Agent Walls."

Walls' face remained stern. "It's no joke, ma'am."

"Let me explain something to you, Walls. I have two weapons that are my personal firearms. One I have on me, as you can see. The other is in my desk drawer. If you care to look, you'll find it there. But that doesn't matter since both are military issue and are not registered in the public system. So, whatever weapon you found at the scene isn't mine."

"Can I reach into my pocket without getting shot, General?"

Thurston nodded. "Go ahead."

He reached into his coat pocket and as he did so, said, "I have two pieces of paper, ma'am. One is a copy of a registration form with your name and signature. The other is a warrant for your arrest."

Thurston took the paper and stared at it, paying particular attention to the signature at the bottom. Ferrero took the warrant and looked it over. He then glanced at the FBI agent and said, "This murder took place last night, Agent Walls? Is that correct?"

Ferrero knew it was.

"Yes."

"Then you might as well stop right there. The general has been with us all the time. We've been running an operation for the past few days, and none of us have been off base."

"I have my orders."

Ferrero looked at Thurston. "Mary?"

She looked up at him. "This is my signature, but

I don't know how it got here."

"Say the word, General, and we'll run these guys out of El Paso."

Thurston shook her head. "No, I'll go with them. It won't take long. Luis, you'll be in charge—"

"No, he won't."

Heads turned to see a newcomer standing in the doorway. He had gray hair and a lined face and wore a dark suit. "I'm going to be taking over while the general is indisposed."

"Who are you?" Thurston asked.

"Norman Holdsworth. I've been sent from Washington to oversee this operation."

"You're not needed," Thurston said curtly. "Luis can run things in my absence."

"This is not a democracy, General. You've been relieved of command forthwith. I am now in charge."

They all looked at one another, unsure of what to do. Thurston broke the silence. "Luis, take my sidearm. Walls, let's get this over and done with so I can get back here."

Ferrero walked over to the general and leaned in to extract her M17. As he did so, she whispered, "Tell Hank."

"Yes, ma'am."

With that done, Walls moved in to put handcuffs on her. "You won't need them, Agent Walls. I will not give you any trouble."

Ferrero watched as they escorted her from the

room, then turned to Holdsworth. "If it's all right with you, we'll get back to work."

"What exactly are you doing?" he asked.

Ferrero told him. Holdsworth nodded and said, "That will cease. The United States Government has men and women especially for that task. You shall concentrate on what you were formed for: bad men with drugs. I expect a brief on my desk at the end of the day, outlining possible targets. Is that understood?"

"Yes, sir."

"Good. If someone will show me where General Thurston's office is?"

"Brooke, show him where to go."

Before they left the ops room, Holdsworth shared one more warning. "Just so you know, I'll not stand for insubordination. Do I make myself clear?"

"Yes, sir."

"Good."

Ferrero waited until Holdsworth was gone before calling Traynor over to him. "Follow the FBI to the airport. I don't like this. It's a fucking setup, and I can't figure out why."

"Do you think it's a coincidence that this guy turns up and puts the investigation we're working on to bed?"

Ferrero shook his head. "No, which is why I need to find out where he's from. Now, go."

Traynor hurried out of the room. Next, Ferrero went over to Swift. The tech said, "He's a bit of a cock, as Knocker would say."

"I agree. Listen, I need you to put together a target package for an op."

"Which one?"

"I don't care; make it the fuck up. Anything to keep Holdsworth off our backs. I'm going to reroute Kane and the others to West Virginia. Actually, make that your target package."

"There is a small band of dope growers up one of the hollows there."

"Good, use that, but keep working on the current mission. Got it?"

"Will do."

"And find out where Bright Spark calls home. I want to know where they have their training base."

"On it."

With that done, Ferrero went to his workstation. He picked up the phone and placed a call to Hank Jones in Washington.

"He fucking what?"

"He's taken over and stopped our investigation."

"What cock-sucking idiot gave him that authorization?" Jones growled.

"I don't know, sir, but I smell a rat," Ferrero told him.

"A dead rodent at that. Well, let's let the rat run a while. I'll monitor things from this end."

"Yes, sir."

Ferrero's next call was to Kane. "I'm rerouting you to West Virginia, Reaper. You should be on the ground there in eight hours."

"What the hell is going on, Luis?" Kane asked.

"I'm not sure. Just keep your head down, and I'll update you as things happen. I'm going to need to do a recon on the Bright Spark base of operations once we nail it down. Also, once we've located Rosalie Spalding, maybe a snatch and grab."

"What about your new friend?" Kane asked.

"You leave him to me."

"Roger that."

———

Ten minutes after leaving the WDI HQ, the two FBI vehicles were trying to cut their way through heavy traffic and getting nowhere. Thurston sat in the back seat, running scenarios through her head. She'd come to the conclusion that this was a ploy to sideline her and her team. As for the new commander coming in to take her position, it was too convenient. It had to be the Cabal.

"Is traffic always this bad at this time of the day?" Walls asked her.

Thurston frowned. Come to think of it, the traffic was never this thick on this road at any time. Then she saw why—up ahead were workmen who had the street cordoned off and were diverting vehicles around what appeared to be a worksite.

"Take the next left," she snapped at Walls.

He turned his head to look at her. "Why?"

"Because this isn't right."

"What are you talking about?"

"There is no roadwork in the El Paso area in the daytime," Thurston explained. "Only at night unless it's an emergency. It was a law brought in last year."

Walls shrugged. "Maybe it is an emergency."

"I'm telling you, there's something wrong."

They drove past the next intersection without turning and Thurston went silent, concentrating on looking for threats. She could see seven workmen doing various jobs as the SUV crept along. One of them dropped from view as the first FBI vehicle blocked her line of sight.

"Keep your eyes on the workmen, Walls," Thurston urged him.

"You worry too much. You're starting to sound like a crackpot conspiracy theorist," he said, dismissing her concerns.

Suddenly the driver in the lead SUV slammed on his brakes and brought the vehicle to an abrupt stop. The driver in the next one followed suit, trying to avoid a collision, and a curse escaped his lips. Through the window, Thurston saw one of the workers drop his road sign and she could hear a *POP-POP* in the distance.

Continuing to watch the workman who'd dropped his sign, she saw him bring up MP7 and shouted, *"Gun!"*

CHAPTER 15

Thurston sank down in the back seat as the shooter began spraying the SUV with automatic fire. Bullets hammered into the front quarter panel and the hood. The windshield shattered, and the driver jerked with a yell as rounds punched into his body.

Walls dropped low, trying to find shelter as more bullets peppered the vehicle. "We have to get out of here," Thurston shouted at the FBI agent. "Move."

She flung the rear door open and slid out onto the asphalt, taking shelter behind the vehicle as bullets sprayed in her direction. Several heartbeats passed as she waited for the shooter's gun to run dry, and when he started changing out the magazine, she closed her door and opened the driver's.

The dead man fell halfway of the vehicle out as she flung the door wide. Ignoring the blood and ghastly wounds, she searched under his coat for a handgun and found a Glock. She checked the load.

The shooter had finished reloading and started firing once more. Thurston scooted toward the rear of the SUV and slid behind it. Walls was there trying to gather himself, shocked at the severity and suddenness of the attack. Weapon in hand, he leaned out and fired twice before pulling back and saying, "Looks like you were right. Fuck!"

The general followed suit on her side of the SUV, firing at the man with the MP7. Her shots forced him to take cover, but Thurston swore because her shots had missed. She waited, Glock raised, for the shooter to reappear. When he did, she fired once. Her aim was perfect, and the bullet punched into the man's face.

She ducked back quickly, and for the first time, noticed the panicked civilians who'd abandoned their vehicles and were running for cover.

"General! General Thurston!"

She looked around for the voice and saw Traynor crouching beside a Tahoe. Keeping low, he rushed to her side, an M17 in his hand. "What happened?"

"We got hit by shooters dressed as workmen. I think they were after me."

"Then let's get you out of here," the ex-DEA man told her.

Thurston nodded. "Walls! We need to move."

He looked across at her as he reloaded his weapon. "What? Where did he come from?"

"No time for that. Follow us."

"What about my men?" he protested.

"They're gone," Thurston told him. "Now, move or die. Your choice."

She and Traynor started back along the vehicles until they reached the one Traynor had tailed them in. The general turned to look for Walls and saw that he'd chosen to come with them and was not far behind. "Get in," she ordered.

After they climbed in, Traynor behind the wheel, he started the SUV and reversed as far as he could before turning into the opposite lane. They rocketed back the way they'd come, then Thurston said, "Take the next turn."

"Where are we going?" the ex-DEA man asked.

"I still have a plane to catch."

"You're seriously still going, ma'am?" Traynor asked incredulously. "Those guys were after you. They could have more on the other end."

"I'll call Hank Jones once we're in the air. He'll send help."

"Would someone tell me what the fuck just happened and why they are after you, as you just said?"

"It's a long story," the general answered.

"I just lost my whole fucking team."

Thurston nodded grimly and said, "All right, I'll tell you."

"What the hell happened?" Ferrero asked when Traynor returned.

"They drove straight into an ambush," he explained.

"I figured as much when reports started coming in. Where is the general?"

"She's on her way to Washington," Traynor replied.

"What?"

"The general figures she needs to get things sorted out at that end. Maybe find some answers while she's at it."

"Good-fucking-grief. What if they're waiting for her on that end?"

"She thought that might be a possibility, so she called ahead to get some help."

"I still don't like it. All right, leave it with me."

They were about to go their separate ways when Holdsworth appeared. "Where have you been, Mister Traynor?"

"Out running errands, Mister Holdsworth," he replied insolently.

The man stared at him suspiciously. "From now on, anyone who leaves the building comes to me first. Understood?"

Before anyone could answer, he continued. "How is that target package coming along?"

Ferrero looked at Swift. The tech looked up from his computer and said, "It's just about done."

"Good. And the team?"

"A few more hours yet. I'm rerouting them to

West Virginia."

An uncertain expression flitted across Holdsworth's face before disappearing. "Why?"

"That's where our next target is."

"What target?"

"A bunch of backwoods hicks have a dope empire up in the mountains," Ferrero explained. "We'll clean them out."

"I'd have thought dope-growing country folk would be a bit below this team?"

"No job too big or too small."

Holdsworth nodded. "I want that brief on my desk as soon as it's done."

"Yes, sir."

When he was gone, Ferrero turned to Swift. "Give me something."

"Well, I think I have two somethings."

Ferrero nodded. "Speak."

"Rosalie Spalding just poked her head up in Washington, along with a man we assume is Darius. Cameras caught her transiting Dulles. The second is that Rogers has a camp in Kentucky. In the Daniel Boone National Forest, in fact."

Ferrero frowned. "How does that work?"

"In 2013, the government realized the public was getting tired of the constant revolving door of troops circulating through the Middle East, so more tasks were allocated to private contractors. Bright Spark quickly grew to be the biggest, and their original base in Montana wasn't large enough. They put it to the government that they would purchase some of the Daniel Boone Forest to set up another base. Plenty of secluded places for them to use. Given the government's debt, a simple way to raise revenue was to sell off assets, so it was agreed upon."

"They can't fly planes out of there," Traynor pointed out.

"They don't need to. They have an airbase in Texas and another in California. The bases in Kentucky and Montana are used to train their men."

"Just how many men do they have?"

"About two battalions."

Ferrero's eyebrows went up. "Sixteen hundred men?"

Swift shrugged. "Give or take."

"Shit. See if you can track Rosalie Spalding's movements. I'll send Knocker to Washington, and he can help the general. The others can head into the Daniel Boone Forest and do a recon mission."

———

"What happened?" Holdsworth asked Rogers.

"Sometimes things go that way," was the response.

"It was set up perfectly, and now the incident will draw unwanted attention."

"It'll be taken care of. What happened on your end?"

"Nothing. I have them focused on a new mission."

"Where?" Rogers asked.

"In West Virginia."

"Find out where. I can have a team on the ground within an hour of them getting there. They won't know what hit them."

"I'll do it."

Rogers disconnected and left Holdsworth with his thoughts. The Cabal had trusted him with a lot. To dismantle the WDI from within was going to be a tough task, especially with Jones and the President in the picture. If he could shift their focus for even a moment, it would make things easier. The destruction of the field team would do that, as well as the war in Colombia. Although the mission to eliminate the team in Colombia had failed, he had no reason to doubt that they would send another party.

Then his contact in the Justice Department could go to work and disassemble the rest, holding those in charge, except for him, responsible, citing a lack of good judgment or whatever else it took.

Somewhere over the Continental United States

Kane answered the satellite phone and found Ferrero on the other end. "What's up?"

"I have a mission for you and your team, minus one."

"Which one?"

"Knocker. I want to send him to Washington to help the general," Ferrero explained. "She'll need it."

"Roger that. What do you want us to do?"

Ferrero told him, and Kane came back with, "We'll need a few things. ISR, ammo resupply, and UAV cover. Cara will need a CSASS. Actually, send us some HK 417s. We could use the extra hitting power."

Where their usual 416s fired a 5.56 round, the 417 cut loose a 7.62. The rate of fire went down a little, but the stopping power of the 417 was far greater.

"Anything else?" Ferrero asked.

"Get clearance for Coles and his Delta team to stay with us. No one knew they were in Colombia, so they aren't compromised."

"I'll get it."

"Have our air assets on standby somewhere close. If this goes sideways, we're going to need a fast extract."

"By the time you touch down, I'll have everything organized. Take care, Reaper."

"Roger that."

The call disconnected, and Kane looked around the cargo bay of the C-130. He got everyone's attention, and they congregated around a large crate in the center. "You look like things just went to shit," Cara observed.

"Maybe they did. There's been some new developments."

Axe groaned. "'Developments.' That's the code word for 'Something's gone to shit somewhere in the world and we'll end up in the middle of it, trying to keep from taking a dirt nap.'"

"Someone took a shot at the general. Traynor managed to get her out of the predicament, along with a Feeb. The rest of the FBI team was KIA."

There was a mutter from the team before Kane continued, "When we get off the plane in West Virginia, we should have fresh ammo and other goodies waiting for us. Including 417s."

"Why?" Cara asked, sensing she wasn't going to like the answer.

"I'll get to that." He turned his gaze on the SAS man. "Knocker, you'll be going to Washington to help keep the general safe."

He nodded. "I don't mind skiving off somewhere good."

Kane looked at Coles. "You guys up for a bit of extra activity? We could use your help."

Coles nodded. "Just point us in the right direction and turn us loose."

"Thanks," Kane replied. "We're going to slip into Kentucky on a little recon mission. Bright Spark has a training camp there, so we're going to have a look around."

"How many hostiles?" Brick asked.

"Roughly a battalion."

Brick gave him a funny look, then realized Kane

wasn't kidding. "This is going to be grand."

Knocker smiled. "You see that? I'm a positive influence on the team."

"Hence the 417s," Cara theorized.

"Yeah. Plus, UAV cover and air support on stand-by for extract."

Axe gave them a wry grin. "I'm getting a hard-on."

"Keep it away from me, stud," Cara warned him.

Kane looked at Coles. "You still in?"

"Ain't got nowhere else to be."

"All right, then. Let's get our gear sorted out. When we get off this plane, I want everyone carrying. You all know what we're up against. I don't want to be surprised if they're waiting for us."

CHAPTER 16

Worldwide Drug Initiative, El Paso, Texas

"Where's that damned workup for the mission I'm waiting for?" Holdsworth demanded.

Ferrero picked up a manila folder from the desk. "I'm sorry, sir. I meant to bring it in, but I got waylaid by something else."

"I hope you don't run your operations like that, Mister Ferrero. I might have to replace you if this tardiness continues."

"Yes, sir."

Holdsworth snatched the folder from Ferrero's grasp and opened it. "Is everything here?"

"Yes, sir."

"And the team?"

"On the ground in the staging area as we speak," Ferrero replied. Which was true.

"Good. What is their ETA on target?"

Ferrero stared at him for a moment. *This guy is ex-military.* "Around zero one hundred, sir. They'll move in at dawn."

"Fine, fine. I gather everything is done through live feed, yes?"

Ferrero nodded. "Where possible."

"OK. That will be all."

"Yes, sir."

Holdsworth studied the folder for a few more moments, then disappeared into his newly acquired office. Ferrero hurried over to Swift and said, "You got it?"

"I soon will have if he makes a call."

"What if he uses a burner?"

Swift gave him a wicked smile. "Nothing gets out of these walls without my knowing."

Ferrero stared at him for a moment before saying, "Remind me to fire you when this is done."

The computer tech chuckled and went back to work.

———

"I have everything you need. I'll send it through."

"Good," Rogers replied. "Do it now so I can get my team in the field."

"It'll be there directly," Holdsworth said. "Don't fuck it up this time. You wouldn't be the first lieutenant replaced by the Cabal."

"Speak for yourself."

The line went dead.

"We got him," Swift said to Ferrero. "Oh, boy, do we got him. Listen to this."

The computer tech played the recording of the phone conversation and waited. Ferrero looked at him and nodded. "What we have, Mister Swift, is a big fish. Good work."

"Does this mean you're not going to fire me?"

"I'd kiss you, except they have rules about that these days."

"I'll settle for a beer."

"Done. Give me a copy of that recording."

"Hey, *amigos*, what is happening?"

Ferrero looked up and saw Arenas limping across the room toward him. "What are you doing here, Carlos?"

"Came to get a couple of things and maybe give you an answer to your offer about helping out with ops planning."

"You in or out?"

Arenas stared at him, curious about the clipped sentences. "I'm in."

"Good. Get a gun and come with me. Pete, you too."

"You'll need this, Boss," Swift said, handing Ferrero the thumb drive.

He put it in his pocket, and the three men walked with purpose from the room.

Looking up from studying the folder on the desk in front of him, Holdsworth glared at the man who'd just intruded in his office. Alarm flickered across his face as he realized something was terribly wrong. Still… "What is the meaning of this?" he blustered.

"It's over, Holdsworth. We know who you are."

"What are you on about?"

"You work for the Cabal."

God, he had been worried about Rogers, and it was going to be him. "What?"

Ferrero walked around the desk and plugged in the thumb drive to the computer. He then clicked a couple of icons with the mouse, and the telephone call played back.

"Deny it."

Holdsworth's face paled. "Oh, good God."

"That about sums it up."

"I'm a dead man."

"I wouldn't go that far."

"You don't understand," he blurted. "As soon as they discover I'm compromised, they'll have me killed."

"Who?"

"Does it matter? You can never reach them."

"Who, damn it?" Ferrero snapped.

For the ex-military man, he figured Holdsworth to be, Ferrero was surprised that getting an answer out of him wasn't tougher. The imposter said, "The inner circle. Ares."

"Who are they?" Ferrero demanded. "Who is the inner circle?"

Holdsworth shook his head.

"Is Rogers Ares?"

"No."

"Who is Ares?"

"I don't know."

Ferrero tried again. "Who's the inner circle?"

Another shake of the head.

"How many?"

"Four."

"Who?"

Silence.

"Come on, Holdsworth, who is the inner circle?"

More silence.

Ferrero paused. "What does Rogers do?"

He looked at the operations officer. "He's their army."

"I figured that out already. Is he inner circle?"

Holdsworth nodded jerkily. "Yes."

"Who else?"

No answer.

"Was Spalding inner circle?" Ferrero asked.

The question registered. "No."

"What was he, then?"

"A patriot."

Traynor snorted derisively. "What kind of patriot kills their own to start a war?"

Holdsworth's eyes flared. "Nothing we do is to the detriment of our country."

"We?" asked Ferrero. "Are you inner circle too?"

His shoulders slumped. "What does it matter? I'm dead anyway. Yes, I'm inner circle."

"How many more?"

"Two more."

"Who are they?"

Silence.

"What's your real name?"

Holdsworth looked at Ferrero. "Does it matter? When you work in the shadows, what's in a name?"

"What's the one your mother gave you?"

His expression changed. "You have to protect her," he said urgently.

"Who?"

"My daughter and her children."

Ferrero nodded slowly. "All right. We can help you, but you have to help us."

"You don't understand. They'll kill them if they think I talked."

"We can keep them safe."

"No one is safe. Look what happened to Marc Spalding."

"The Cabal killed him?" Ferrero asked.

"Yes."

"Who?"

"Rogers. We'd already decided it needed to be done, but it was brought forward by Ares."

"Who is Ares?"

"I don't know. We haven't met him."

"You carry out orders given to you by a man you've never met?"

"Only one of the inner circle has ever met him, and he won't say."

"Who?"

"Clive Rogers."

"Where does your daughter live?"

"Saint Louis. If I don't send the information soon, they'll know something's wrong," Holdsworth warned them.

"OK, send it. But if you try anything funny, I'll leave your daughter in the breeze just long enough for the Cabal to find her and the kids."

While Holdsworth typed on the computer in front of him, Ferrero said to Traynor, "Send word to Kane. Tell him he's about to have visitors, and I'll send him more intel when it comes to hand."

Traynor left the room, and Holdsworth looked up from the computer. "There. It's done. Rogers will send his men to where I've indicated."

"Good."

"And you'll take care of my daughter?"

"Where in Saint Louis?"

He gave Ferrero the address.

"We'll take care of it."

"Thank you."

He gave Ferrero a strange look before opening

the desk's top drawer, his hand coming out filled with a SIG handgun, which he brought up.

"No!" Ferrero yelled, but it was no use.

The M17 in Arenas' hand boomed twice in the small room, and Holdsworth jerked under the impacts. Red appeared on his chest as he slumped in the chair, and the weapon fell from his grasp.

"Son of a bitch!" the operations commander exclaimed.

"Nothing else I could do, Luis," Arenas said apologetically.

"It's not your fault, Carlos. He knew they'd get to him."

The door flew open and Traynor and Reynolds stormed in, guns in hand. "Take it easy," Ferrero said. "It's over."

Allegheny Mountains, West Virginia

The team moved slowly through the stretch of eastern hemlock, sweeping left and right as they went. The sun was almost down, and the dimness of the forest made it particularly hard to detect anything that might be classed as a threat. Kane checked the team's coordinates and knew they still had at least one more klick to cover before reaching their area of operation.

According to Ferrero, the location had been

passed to Clive Rogers, the CEO of Bright Spark, who was sending a team to intercept them. Team Reaper's involvement was a way of confirming Rogers' connection to the Cabal.

With that done, they could move on Rogers. He sensed Cara coming up behind him. He turned. "How much farther, Dan'l Boone?"

"Another klick."

She was about to reply when gunfire erupted up on point. A voice screamed through their comms, *"Contact front! Contact front. Man down! Man down!"*

Kane pressed his talk button. "Roger that. We're on our way."

———

The call had come from Coles. He and another of his men, a corporal named Tyler, had volunteered to take point and had walked into a wall of bullets from a hidden force. Starting with a shattered leg, Tyler was then struck from the side, the shot missing his body armor and piercing his chest as he was collapsing from the first wound. Coles dropped to the ground and made the emergency transmission, then he felt bullets impacting all around him and the hot air from their passage close to his face.

"Motherfucker," he cursed out loud as he slithered toward his wounded man. He knew that he should be returning fire, but he was exposed, and to attempt to rise and fire would invite a bullet through his head. Instead, he concentrated on dragging his man into a piece of bowl-shaped ground to his right.

"Hang in there, Tye," he growled. "Help is on the way, buddy."

Once they were in the depression, Coles brought his HK 417 up into the firing position. They too had swapped their weapons out for the harder-hitting assault rifle. With the firing selector set to semi, he began shooting back, praying that help wasn't too far away. "Hang in there, Tye," he muttered again. "Hang in there."

———

Kane and the others covered the ground between them and the firing line as fast as they could. Coles and Tyler had been three hundred meters in front of the main group as they scouted the terrain ahead.

To his left, he could see high ground, which the team could possibly use. He called as he ran, "Cara, Axe, the high ground to the left. Set up there with the SAW and the CSASS. Make sure you can get a good field of fire. The rest of you, on me."

Cara and Axe diverted from the trail and jogged up the hemlock-covered slope. Even after they'd made the ridge, they could see nothing. "On me, Axe," Cara called and ran along the rock-strewn spine. Fifty meters farther on, it fell away, and she stopped. Axe joined her, and they took in the situation before them. From what they could see, the shooters were spread out in a half-moon shape cutting the trail, with each end curled in so they could fire from the flanks. What they hadn't counted on was the team's point being so far ahead of the main element.

Now, with the enemy having shown their hand, the team had the opportunity to hit them where it hurt.

"Reaper One, copy?"

"Read you Lima Charlie, Reaper Two."

"The shooters are in the shape of a half-moon across the trail. Suggest you flank right and roll them up from that side. I count ten…no, thirteen shooters. One of them has a SAW in the center."

"Roger that. Will adjust accordingly. Out."

Beside Cara, Axe set up his SAW and waited. He looked at her. "Wasn't this supposed to be the other way around?"

"One would have thought so," she replied, then, "Reaper, let me know when you're in position."

Down below, Cole fired at any target that presented itself. So far, he'd accounted for one shooter and been hit himself, the pain from the wound radiating up his left arm. As luck would have it, it was little more than a scratch. Still, it hurt like a bitch.

"Reaper One, Delta One. Where are you guys?" Cole hissed as he changed out a magazine and slapped a fresh one home.

"Hang in there, Delta One. We're almost with you."

A round cracked close, and Cole dropped his head to the ground. The scent of damp earth filled his nostrils, reminding him of better times as a child, playing at war with his brothers on the farm, crawling through the grass. Now they were all real and people died. He glanced at Tyler and saw that he'd stopped moving. "Shit. Hold on, buddy."

Meanwhile, Kane and the others were circling around to get behind the shooters. Once they were in position, he radioed Cara. "Reaper Two, copy?"

"Roger, Reaper."

"When I give the word, you and Axe open fire on the shooters. That'll give us a chance to take them by surprise from behind. Just watch your fire."

"Copy."

"All right. Three, two, one, execute."

From his position, Kane heard the SAW open fire with its staccato rhythm. In between, he heard Cara's single shots with the sniper system she was using. He counted to ten in his head and then said, "All call signs move forward. Terminate all targets."

Kane and the others stood and moved forward cautiously, picking off targets with trained precision. By the time the private contractors realized what was happening, it was too late. The last one went down with a Delta man's bullet in his head.

"Cease fire! Cease fire!" Kane ordered into his comms. "Brick, check on the casualty."

"Roger that."

"Zero, this is Reaper One, copy?"

"Read you Lima Charlie, Reaper."

"Situation contained. What the fuck happened?"

"I have no idea, Reaper. Our intel should have had you walking into a quiet situation."

"It was anything but. We need a medevac inbound. We've got one WIA. I'll relay his status when I know more."

"Roger, standing by."

When Kane approached Cole, the Delta team leader was watching Brick work on his operator. "You OK, Cole?"

Cole turned and nodded. "What the fuck happened? We walked straight into a shitstorm. No one was meant to be here."

"It may not seem like it, but it could have been worse. Without such a large gap between us, it would have been a different story."

"Yeah, maybe you're right."

"Brick, what's his status?"

Without looking up, the combat medic said, "He's priority one, Reaper. We need to get him out ASAP."

"Zero, copy?"

"Go ahead."

"Our WIA is priority one, I say again, priority one."

"Copy, priority one. We've got a bird in the air and headed your way. It's about ten minutes out. Keep me updated."

"Brick, there's a helo about ten mikes out."

"Roger that."

Kane turned to Axe and Cara, who were descending from the ridge. "Axe, check these guys and see what you can dig up. Be quick. Once these assholes miss their check-in, things are going to happen."

A few minutes later, Axe came back to him. "We got nothing. I suspect the comms link they're using has shut down by now too. Probably shut down their link to the satellite they're using."

Kane thought for a moment and then smiled. "Bravo Four, copy?"

"Ten-four, good buddy."

"Shit. Listen, these guys had to be using a satellite for their comms. There is no other way with the terrain like it is. Can you find out which bird they're using and track the feed?"

"I can try, but if it's shut down, I won't get squat."

"See what you can do."

In the distance, the WHOP-WHOP of rotor blades reached out across the mountains as the medevac picked its way through the high valley. The daylight was all but gone, and the first sighting of the bird was its lights through a gap in the trees. "Everyone, switch your strobes on."

"Reaper One, this is Angel One-One, copy?"

"Good copy, Angel One-One. We've got our strobes on, so you should pick us up shortly."

"Roger that. Wait one."

There was a moment of silence before a different voice came back on the channel. "Reaper One, Angel One-Three. What's the status of your WIA? Over."

Kane looked at Brick. The ex-SEAL nodded and came on comms. "Angel One-Three, this is Reaper Five. We have a priority-one medevac. Blood pressure is low, seventy over forty, pulse is fluctuating, I've got plasma hooked into an IV line, which I'm trying to get into him as fast as I can. The casualty has a wound to his thigh and upper left chest. Suspect internal bleeding. Lung was collapsed, but I managed to relieve pressure to the chest cavity."

"Copy, Reaper Five."

"Angel One-One, this is Reaper One."

"Go, Reaper One."

"Listen, there is no clear LZ where we are. Are you rigged to winch?"

"Affirmative, Reaper One."

"Copy. We'll have him ready to go."

CHAPTER 17

Washington, DC

Knocker Jensen slipped the magazine into the suppressed 416 and readied himself to breach the four-story building in front of them. Most of the lights were out inside the main office block of Bright Spark Solutions, but some of the offices were still occupied. Thurston had made the call to do the job, the two of them against a security team tried and tested on the field of battle. When she'd told the SAS man of her decision, he'd given her a broad grin and said, "Just point me in the right direction, General, and turn me loose. We'll hit them hard and kick the buggers in the twigs and berries as we go."

"I'm glad you're confident," she'd said to him.

"Ma'am, us SAS blokes have been cut off, out-numbered, and shit out of luck ever since World War Two. This is what we do."

He tugged his body armor and tapped his magazine pouches, a habit he'd picked up long ago in the Sandbox. He then turned to Thurston, who was dressed like he was in full tactical gear. "You ready, ma'am?"

"As I'll ever be."

"Just stay on my ass."

"This isn't my first rodeo, you know."

"It may be our last, though," he quipped and broke cover, hurrying toward the main entrance.

"Bravo Four, call them as you see them."

"Roger, Reaper Three. You've got two guards at the front door."

"Copy."

Through his NVGs, the laser sights reached out in an unwavering line. It seemed to spear the first of the armed guards at the entrance, and as soon as it did, Knocker stroked the trigger of his carbine twice. The man dropped to the ground and didn't move again. Immediately he switched targets, and before the dead security man's surprised partner could react, two 5.56 rounds punched into his upper body.

"Two tangos down at the front entrance."

"The foyer is clear, Reaper Three. Once you enter, turn left for the elevator. Your targets are on the fourth floor."

"Copy that."

Knocker walked past the dead men on the office block's stoop, lifted his NVGs, and pushed through the large glass door. Following Swift's instructions, he turned left.

The floor was polished tile, and every footfall echoed around the large foyer. Apart from a desk and a couple of potted plants, there was nothing acoustic to absorb the sound.

"Bravo Four, are you sure the security cameras are all down?" Thurston asked.

"As far as I can tell, ma'am. It doesn't mean they won't twig that something is wrong."

They found the lift at the left end of the foyer beside a public bathroom. Knocker hit the button, and the doors slid open. They stepped inside, and he pressed the button for the floor that held their target. With a slight jolt, the elevator began its ascent, a faint whirring audible on the inside. As they slid past the second floor, Swift's voice came over the comms. Instead of a warning, he said, "Oh, shit."

"Speak to me, Slick," Thurston said hurriedly.

"More tangos just appeared on the fourth floor. There are now eight present."

Without hesitation, Knocker slammed his gloved fist on the third-floor button. The elevator stopped, and he started to disembark.

"What are you doing?" Thurston hissed.

"Change of plan, ma'am. I'm not getting out of one kill box into another. Are you coming?"

She stepped off the elevator and followed him. "What about when the elevator pings on the fourth floor and no one gets off?"

"We'll use it to our advantage," he told her, then, "Where's the stairs, Bravo Four?"

"Keep going to the end of the hallway, and it's the door on the right."

"Roger that."

Knocker broke into a jog until he reached the door, Thurston hot on his heels. The SAS man swung the door open and started up the stairs. Just before they reached the landing, he slowed to a stop. "Bravo Four, how are we looking?"

"Exit is clear. They have moved toward the elevator."

Knocker glanced at Thurston and nodded. "Left or right?"

"Left."

He pulled a flashbang from his webbing and said, "Let's go."

Opening the door as far as he dared, Knocker tossed the flashbang into the open plan-office and pulled the door closed. It exploded with a loud *CRUMP*, and the noise doubled as a signal to enter.

Once through the door, Knocker stepped in his prearranged direction while Thurston went in hers, their suppressed weapons up and firing. Two of the eight people inside fell with bullets in them. The remainder dropped to the floor while trying to recover from the blast.

The first one to do so came up holding a handgun. He fired twice at Thurston, who ducked, then came back up and blew three holes in his chest. Three more people appeared, and Knocker recognized two of them: Rosalie Spalding and the man called Darius. He rattled off a couple of shots, and Darius spun around. Rosalie Spalding let out a curse and fired the rest of her magazine at the SAS man in anger.

Drywall dust and debris filled the air with fine silt as bullets punched through the walls. Knocker fired a burst at a shooter and saw him fall. Darius, though wounded, was still in the fight. He rose and blew off four rounds at Thurston, while behind him, the three remaining people, Rosalie included, started to shift position.

"They're moving!" Thurston called to Knocker.

The SAS man swore under his breath as he dropped a spent magazine from the 416 and replaced it with a fresh one. He raised the weapon and aligned its sights on the broad chest of Darius. "Merry fucking Christmas, cock," he grated and put three rounds into the wounded shooter.

Rosalie and the two men with her disappeared through a doorway in the far corner of the open-plan room. Thurston said into her comms, "Bravo Four, we have three rabbits. Confirm one as Rosalie Spalding and the other as Clive Rogers."

Knocker's head spun to look at his commanding officer. "Are you sure?"

"Straight up."

"Ma'am, they're headed down a secondary stairwell that comes out at the rear of the building."

"Copy that. We're going after them."

Knocker led the way. As he passed one of the fallen shooters, who moaned, the SAS man shot him without compunction and continued after their targets.

Upon entering the stairwell, Knocker leaned over the rail to look down. There was nothing to see but the narrow gap that fell away to the ground floor. He began making his descent cautiously but with the confidence of a trained Special Operator. Following him, Thurston had to admit, the more she saw of the SAS man, the more he impressed her.

Toward the bottom, he stopped.

"What is it?" Thurston asked.

He shook his head. "I don't know. There's been no noise."

"Keep moving?"

Once they reached the bottom, he stopped and tried the door, which was locked. He flipped the latch and stopped once again. "Now what?" the general asked in frustration.

"The door was locked."

"So?"

"From the inside."

Understanding the ramifications, she spun and raised her carbine, pointing it back up the stairs. The escapes hadn't come this way. There was no way they could have used the door and locked it from the inside. "Bravo Four," Knocker said. "Does ISR show our three runners to be anywhere inside the building?"

"Negative, Reaper Three."

"Well, they fucking went somewhere, man. Take a fucking look."

"Easy, Knocker," Thurston soothed. "We'll find them."

"Is there an exit we don't know about?"

"Not according to the plans we were able to find. One minute they were there and the next they were gone."

"They can't be fucking just gone."

"Would you like to have a look?" Swift asked curtly.

"Well, find them, or I'll come through this fucking comms and feed you your fucking bollocks."

"Knocker!" Thurston snapped. "Cut it, or you'll be without yours. They had to have gone somewhere. If it wasn't down here, it had to be another floor, and the only way off them is via the other stairwell or the elevator. Slick, talk to me."

"They're definitely not in a stairwell," the computer tech told them.

"Shit," Knocker muttered and pushed his way past Thurston to the first floor. Once there, he breached the door and came out in a hall with office doors on either side. When he reached the elevator, the SAS man hit the button. The conveyance whirred and stopped on their floor. The doors slid back, and Knocker stepped in. He stood there and sniffed the air as would a hunting dog looking for its quarry. "You smell it?" he asked Thurston.

She joined him in the elevator and followed suit. Then she smelled it—the scent of the various chemicals from the gun battle upstairs. She looked down at the floor and saw the footprints caused by dust from the shattered drywall. "They were in here."

"Yes. The question is, where did they go?"

He studied at the interior of the elevator closely. Then he stared at the panel.

"What is it?" Thurston asked him, leaning in.

She was so close he could smell her, and for a moment, his mind wandered at the sweetness she radiated. "I think there's something with this panel."

Thurston stepped back and cocked her head to the side. Then she lifted her foot and lashed out, driving her heel against the metal plate.

The plate buckled and sprang open at the bottom to reveal a small compartment with a green button. Knocker nodded. "That'll work."

He pressed it. The doors slid closed, and the elevator started its downward journey. The level ticker hit G for ground and stopped. However, the elevator kept going for another ten seconds before slowing and then gave a small jerk as it too stopped.

The SAS man moved to one side of the elevator before the doors slid open. He raised his 416 and got ready to meet whatever was on the other side head-on.

A cold, empty, concrete hallway ran straight for twenty meters before turning to the right. Knocker and Thurston moved along it, their footsteps echoing with monotonous regularity. Even their breathing seemed to bounce off the lit passageway.

"I guess we know where they went." Knocker's whisper was like a shout.

"Keep it down," Thurston hissed.

He shrugged. "They're long gone, General."

"Keep moving."

Again, he shrugged and did as she ordered. At the end of the corridor, he turned right and followed the hallway a further ten meters to a door. He casually opened it, and they found a small parking garage on the other side.

Thurston cursed and said into her comms. "Bravo Four, copy?"

She was met with nothing but static. "Shit."

"Let's go back and see if we can find anything in the office," Knocker suggested. "Maybe your computer whiz will be able to use something."

"Maybe."

———

"Get us out of the city," Rogers commanded. "Have the helicopter waiting at the designated area."

"Yes, sir," the driver replied curtly.

Rogers turned to Rosalie. "I have to inform Ares of what just happened."

Rosalie nodded. "How did they know?"

"Know what?"

"They came there for one of us," she said. "The West Virginia team has gone dark. Our sources are saying they're all dead. Are they the ones who killed my father?"

"Yes," he lied as he reached for his encrypted cell. He punched in a number and waited.

"What is it?'

"My offices in Washington were just hit."

"By whom?" Ares asked.

"Who the fuck do you think? It had to be the WDI."

Ares sighed. "This is getting very messy, Clive."

"You don't think I know that?" he snapped. "First the West Virginia team, and now this."

"What about the West Virginia team?"

"They've gone dark."

"By dark, you mean they're dead?"

"Maybe."

There was a drawn-out silence before Ares asked, "What did you leave behind?"

"What do you mean?"

"In your offices. What did you leave behind that can point to our organization?"

Rogers thought for a moment. Too long. "Nothing."

"Clive?"

"Nothing, I'm sure of it."

Beside him, Rosalie's cell buzzed. The screen lit up, and she read the message that came through. She tucked it back into her pocket and listened to the conversation between her uncle and Ares.

"I hope for your sake that is true, Clive. The House and Senate voted earlier. The announcement is about to be made. We're going to war."

"My men will be ready."

"I hope so."

The connection went dead.

"Fuck!" Rogers hissed and slammed his fist into the seat of the SUV.

"Is everything OK?" Rosalie asked.

"Just fine," he growled.

She could tell it wasn't. "What is it, Clive?"

"What's this 'Clive' business? What happened to 'Uncle?'"

"What's wrong?"

"I have a hard drive in a safe in the office with a lot of financial stuff on it."

"What kind of financial stuff?" Rosalie asked.

"Overseas accounts, payments made and received, that kind of stuff."

She thought for a moment as the SUV lurched over a bump in the street. "The accounts. Are those all the accounts linked to the company? All of your money?"

"Yes."

"And if they find it and seize the money, you'll be left with nothing?"

"That's about it."

"Is there anything linking payments to the Cabal?"

He snorted derisively. "It all links to the fucking Cabal. Every last cent for the past five years. All they have to do is follow the money."

"Can they trace it to Ares?"

He said nothing.

"Uncle?" Her voice was stern, like she was talking to one of her soldiers back in the day.

"The hard drive also has a list on it. An insurance policy. I knew when I became involved with the Cabal that life was cheap to them, and they could get to anyone they wished. So, I had an insurance policy made to cover my ass if they tried it with me."

"What is on it? What is the list?"

"Everything. The list is everything. Senators, banking executives, business directors, military personnel. Everyone of importance, right up to Ares."

"Fucking *what*?"

"It's all there."

"You mean, you know who Ares is?"

"Yes."

"And it's on the list?"

"Right at the very top."

"We need to get it before they find it."

Rogers shook his head. "No. We need to destroy it."

"How?"

"By destroying the whole building. A drone strike."

"We can get one up inside thirty minutes."

"Do it."

CHAPTER 18

Thurston and Knocker Jensen sifted through the fourth-floor office space and managed to get Swift logged into the network so he could download anything he found remotely interesting. But it wasn't until they found the single office on the west side of the building that things got really interesting.

"Bingo," Knocker. "This is the bee's knees, this is."

"'Bee's knees?'" Thurston queried as she looked around Rogers' office space.

"Awesome."

"Why don't you just say that, then?"

"Why don't you say 'bee's knees?'"

"Shit. See what you can find."

"Bravo Four, hold what you're doing. We've found Rogers' office. He's got a computer here you're going to want to get into."

"Hook me in, ma'am."

While Thurston did that, Knocker went around the office with an eagle eye, studying everything it came across. The one thing that drew his attention was the portrait of George Patton, complete with American flag and ivory-handled sidearm. It stuck out from the wall farther than the paintings of Sheridan, Ulysses S. Grant, and Robert E. Lee.

"What do we have here?" he muttered, pulling on the painting.

It swung to the left, revealing a wall safe. "Well now, this is interesting. Hey, Bravo Four, what are you like at safecracking?"

"Ooh, a new challenge. I like it. Get me a picture."

"Coming up."

Thurston joined Knocker and looked at the safe. "Forget it. We'll never crack it."

"Not necessarily," Swift said. "I think I might be able to get you in."

"Rock on, MacGyver."

"OK, try this. Six, eight, two, four, nine, one, one, five, seven, three, three, zero, one, three."

"You're taking the piss, aren't you?"

"Just try it."

"You'll have to tell me again. I'm not a fucking elephant."

Swift ran through the numbers again, and the SAS man punched them in as he spoke. With a beep, the lock clicked, and he was able to swing the door open. "You're the dog's bollocks and no mistake."

"I'll take that as a compliment."

Inside the safe were passports, papers, and a hard drive. Knocker grabbed it and said, "This looks important."

He took it over to the computer and plugged it in. "Slick, can you read this hard drive I've just plugged in?"

"Let me have a look." There was a pause in the conversation, then he came back to them. "It's decrypting…oops."

"What's oops?" Thurston asked.

"Something just triggered an early warning safety net I set up," he explained.

"What is it?" Thurston asked.

"It's—"

"It's what?"

"A UAV."

"What's it doing, Bravo Four?"

There was silence.

"Bravo Four?"

"Its current route puts it on target to your position," he replied, his voice on edge.

Thurston looked at Knocker. "What did you do?"

He gave her an incredulous look. "Me? I didn't do anything."

"Slick, give me an ETA."

"If it's there to clean up, I would say it'll be within firing range in approximately two minutes."

"We need to get out of here now," Thurston said

forcefully. "Pull that hard drive."

"No!" Swift blurted over their comms.

"Why the hell not?"

"Because it could wipe it altogether. I haven't even cracked the encryption on it yet. Leave it. All we can do is hope we get something off it before the strike happens. Something is better than nothing."

"All right. We're moving."

They ran for the stairwell and started down, hitting only a couple of stairs on each flight. By the time they hit the bottom and ran out into the foyer, time had run out. Swift shouted, *"It's fired! It's fired!"*

"Christ, what a fucking shambles!" Knocker exclaimed as he ran toward a large plate-glass window that separated them from the outside. He brought his 416 up, flipped the selector to auto as he ran, and emptied almost a full magazine into it. It shattered immediately, the falling glass resembling water cascading over a waterfall.

They burst through the opening and out onto the concrete driveway. In the sky, they could hear the missile's approach and knew it was only a matter of milliseconds before impact. They were diving to the ground when the missile hit the third floor of the building.

"You'd better tell me we got it," Thurston gasped as she limped away from the burning building. Behind her, Knocker wiped at a small cut on his forehead as he watched fire consume the partially destroyed building.

"We got something," Swift replied over the comms. "I don't know what it is yet. It could take a while to work through it."

"Well, get your ass into gear and sort it out."

"Yes, ma'am."

The Cessna CitationJet M2 sat on the tarmac, its turbines already idling when the SUV stopped. Rogers and Rosalie climbed out of the vehicle, the latter staring down at her cell. She looked at her uncle and said, "The building was destroyed."

Rogers breathed a sigh of relief. "Thank God for that. If Ares ever found out I had something like that, I'd be as dead as the next person."

They started toward the aircraft, but sensing that his niece wasn't close behind him, Rogers stopped and turned, a sigh of resignation escaping his lips. "So, that's the way it's going to be?"

"It's nothing personal," she replied.

His face screwed up in anger. "Fuck y—"

The Glock in her fist fired twice, and her uncle dropped to the tarmac. She walked forward, shooting him once more in the head.

Rosalie reached into her pocket and pulled out her cell once more. She hit the speed dial button and said, "It's done."

"Good." Ares sounded happy with her, as though she'd passed some kind of test. "Where are you going?"

"Montana."

"I will make sure no one bothers you."

"The men will be ready to leave within the week. Once on the ground, they will move to secure the trizanthium and relieve the forward team already on location."

"When do they leave?"

"The reports I'm getting say American troops will be on the ground in Colombia inside of three days. They will coincide with that timeframe."

"Who will lead them?"

"Someone I trust."

There was a pause before Ares said, "I'm sorry about your uncle."

"It had to be done."

"Yes, a necessary evil, I'm afraid. There is another problem."

Rosalie nodded. "The man who infiltrated the WDI?"

"Yes. He was another of my trusted lieutenants. I have to assume he is either dead or has been turned against us."

"I will find out."

"If he has been turned, he knows about the two lieutenants who are still alive. They need to be dealt with."

"I will have the teams take care of it." She hesitated. "What about me? I have also been compromised."

Ares chuckled. "Rest assured, my dear. If I didn't need you, your name would also be on that list, but you are essential to the operation in Colombia. However, you need to make sure that should there be any trouble, you are not taken alive."

"I can see to that," Rosalie said stoically.

"Good."

The call disconnected and she climbed aboard the Cessna and buckled in, deep in thought. Five minutes later, it rumbled down the runway before picking up its skirts and lifting into the star-filled sky.

CHAPTER 19

Worldwide Drug Initiative HQ, El Paso, Texas
Two Days Later

"Talk to me, Mary," Hank Jones said over the secure line. "What do you have?"

"Not a lot at the moment, I'm afraid, sir. As you know, Clive Rogers is dead. We assume he was killed because of his indiscretion."

"His fuck-up, you mean. Say it how it is."

"Yes, sir."

"We need something, Mary," Jones growled. "Airborne troops will be on the ground fighting and dying this time tomorrow if you don't."

"That soon?"

"Yes. What did your man get off that hard drive?"

"At the moment, it's just a bunch of numbers. It was somehow corrupted when it downloaded and was disconnected in the blast."

"What about the gunny?"

"He and his team are on standby. If we could—"

The door to Thurston's office flew open, and Swift filled the void. "I found something."

———————

The operations room was filled with the whole of the WDI staff. On the split big screen were Hank Jones to the left and the intel retrieved from the hard drive on the right. Swift was briefing them on what he'd found.

"At first, it was a real bitch to crack, but after I ran a couple hundred algorithms, I finally came across something that worked. It's not much, and it's fractured, but I've been able to run down most of the leads. There is still a lot more to decipher, but what we have now is a good start."

The screen changed, and he continued, "Rogers, from what I can gather, had himself an insurance policy with a heap of names on it. I've been able to crack some of them but not all. We will probably never be able to get them all anyway. I'll put up on your screen, General, what I have so far."

Jones grunted impatiently and stared at the monitor in front of him, face stoic. Then he looked at the camera. "This is going to fuck up someone's day. I see at least five senators on this list who pushed for the war in Colombia, and those men have a lot of influence over the rest of the lawmakers."

"I've yet to run down all the names, but there are some military personnel on it as well, albeit retired."

"I see some names on there that aren't American," Jones pointed out.

"Yes, sir. The one that stands out is Amadou Tigana."

Jones nodded. "I've heard that name. Something to do with a coup in a small African country a couple of years back."

"Yes, sir. Word on the ground at the time was that mercenaries were training and fighting alongside his troops. Bright Spark Solutions was reportedly supplying said mercenaries."

"Son of a bitch."

"That's not all. You'll see the fifth name on the list, Solomon Harris."

"Mining magnate out of Nevada."

"Yes, sir. After the coup was over, he was the first foreigner to put mining equipment on the ground in-country. Actually, he was the only one. Made billions."

"Wait a minute," Hanks said. "I remember now. Isn't Tigana dead?"

"Yes, sir. He was killed in a car bombing last year. Prior to that, he'd been bowing to public pressure from those starting to turn against his regime for allowing the country's main source of wealth to go to foreign investors. Mainly Harris."

"So, the Cabal killed him."

"That would be my guess." A new voice joined

them, and a separate video feed came to life, revealing CIA Director Melissa Smith. "Sorry I'm late."

"What do you know about this, Melissa?"

"The CIA suspected the Cabal had been doing things like this for a while. This is the closest anyone has come, and I think it's scaring them."

"Is this enough to stop the invasion of Colombia, General?" Thurston asked.

"It's supposition at best. All we have is a list of names."

Melissa said, "If you allow me, General, I will put some of my most trusted people on it and see if I can tie names to events."

"All right, do it. What's the rest of the stuff you were able to unlock?"

"Bank accounts with something in the order of thirty billion dollars tied up in them collectively."

"Freeze them. That'll get them thinking."

"Even if we do, I don't think it will matter much. The Cabal, as we've seen, is global. I estimate they collectively have trillions of dollars behind them. I was able to find government officials from at least five different countries on the list."

"What countries?" Jones demanded.

"Germany, Britain, Belgium, France, and Italy," Swift replied.

"What could their end game be?" Jones asked.

Melissa Smith answered, "Global domination."

"What kind of sick asshole wants that?"

"Ares," Kane said, speaking for the first time.

"Ares is the Greek God of war. They use war to achieve their endgame."

"OK, so in Colombia, they get the trizanthium out of that deal. What do they do next?"

Thurston spoke next, "Melissa, you said they would use it for body armor."

"Yes, for a possible upcoming war with either China or Russia."

"Would they force the issue?" Jones asked.

"If you mean start a war with them, I guess it's possible."

Jones swore. "We have to keep them from getting their hands on the trizanthium."

"The only way to do that is to stop the invasion of Colombia," Kane pointed out.

"Even if you do, they'll still find a way," Melissa told them. "It'll only slow them down."

"It'll be a start until we can come up with a way to stop them," Jones said. "I'll take it to the President."

"In the meantime, we'll see if we can find out where Rosalie Spalding is," Thurston informed him. "I have a feeling she'll be filling her uncle's shoes."

"If you find her, take her off the board," Jones growled.

"She may be a wealth of intel, General," Melissa pointed out.

"All right, bring her in. And find out who the hell Ares is. If we can identify him, maybe we can cut the head off the snake."

The feed to Jones went dark and Axe said, "Why do I get the feeling we're about to walk into a whole world of hurt?"

"Cheer up, old cock," Knocker said. "It could be worse."

"Call me a cock again and I'll cut yours off," Axe growled.

Knocker smiled.

"Slick, freeze the money, and get back to finding Rosalie Spalding."

"I'm working on that as we speak."

"How so?"

"I tried to track the plane we assume she got on because of where Rogers' body was found, but there were no flight plans filed, which made it tricky. That meant trolling through a shitload of satellite feeds, and I wasn't about to do that, so I asked myself—"

"Sometime today, Slick," Kane interrupted. "Did you find her?"

"No."

"Shit."

"I think I know where she might be, though."

"Where?"

"Montana. There's been a lot of movement up there over the past few days. Maybe they're getting ready to deploy."

"What about Kentucky?"

"Yes, but if you were her, where would you rather be?"

Thurston nodded. "All right, let's take the chance. Reaper, get your team ready. You're going to Montana."

Kane turned to Arenas, who was seated to one side. "Carlos, you want to work on a target package while we get ready?"

Arenas nodded. "*Sí*. I'll get what I can."

Kane patted him on the shoulder. "It's good to have you back, my friend."

"It is good to be here, even if—"

"Don't sweat it. We can't kick doors all our lives."

"I will put the package together."

An hour later, while the team was putting the finishing touches on their gear, Arenas entered the cage. Cara walked over, wrapped her arms around him, and gave him a kiss on the cheek. "I wish you were coming with us."

"So do I," Knocker said. "I for one don't fancy taking on a flamin' battalion of Ares' warriors."

"I'm sure you will all be fine."

He started to brief them on the target, placing satellite pictures on top of a crate for them to see. "Where did you get these on short notice?" Kane asked him.

"Slick."

"Uh-huh."

"This is the compound they use for their training. It covers at least ten square kilometers.

They selected a good place for the base because it contains some difficult terrain, which will operate to your advantage. To the east is a large rock formation on a ridge. It should be a good place to set up an OP. It also offers Cara a good sniper's nest."

"What about air support?" Kane asked.

"There will be a Gray Eagle on station by dawn. It will be fully armed. Now I'm going to see if I can get you some backup."

"What kind of backup?"

"Whatever I can scrape together. As you can see, you'll be inside their perimeter. If it all goes to the wall, you'll need help."

Arenas continued to brief them on what they needed to know. Once he was done, he said, "Remember, this is only a recon unless you're told otherwise. If the target is onsite, you'll work up a plan to extract her. Understood?"

Kane looked at him and smiled. "You're starting to sound like my father."

"Someone has to keep an eye on your asses. If I'm going to do this job, it's going to be done right. I don't want anything going wrong that could have been foreseen."

Kane nodded. "Let's go to work."

The White House, Washington, DC

"Mister President, you need to turn off the invasion of Colombia."

"I'll need a reason to even consider it, Hank," Carter replied.

Jones gave him more than one. After he finished, Carter asked, "You're sure about all that?"

"As sure as I can be."

"Who do your people think this Ares person is?"

"We don't know, sir. But they will find out eventually."

"All right, I'll pull the troops back. I'll leave the option on the table, though. Do you have the list with you?"

"Yes, sir."

Jones passed it to him, and Carter looked it over. "I know all the senators on this list and many others."

"I figured you would, sir."

"All right, leave it with me. Are you available for a meeting this afternoon? Say, in an hour?"

"Yes, sir."

"Fine. That'll be all."

"Thank you for your time, sir."

Jack Carter watched Jones leave his office before he reached for the cell in his desk drawer. He punched in a number and said, "We have a problem."

Worldwide Drug Initiative HQ, El Paso, Texas

"Ma'am, could I have a word in private?"

Thurston and Ferrero looked curiously at each other, then the ex-DEA agent said, "I'll just be over here."

"What is it?" the general asked her tech.

"I was digging into Rogers' background, and I came up with something troubling."

He held out a picture for her to take. Thurston looked at it and then back at Swift. "Well?"

"If you look at the man in the front row center, you'll see Clive Rogers. Now look at the man next to him. His commanding officer."

Thurston frowned, then tilted her head to one side. "You've got to be fucking shitting me."

"My reaction too, ma'am."

"How can this be?"

"We knew it went deep."

"But that deep?"

"I'm not saying that is Ares, but it sure would fit."

Thurston was stunned.

"What do we do, ma'am?"

"Continue the current mission. Once it's completed, I'll…shit, I don't know."

Thurston went into her office and put a call through to Melissa Smith. "I need to see you now."

"What is it?"

"I'll tell you about it when you get here."

"I've got meetings I need to get to, Mary."

"I think we've found out who Ares is."

"I'll be there in a few hours."

Washington, DC, in the Air

The Gulfstream G500 had begun to climb after takeoff and Melissa Smith stared out the window, wondering what or who Ares was. The runway fell behind the aircraft, and she felt a shudder from turbulence as it clawed higher. Even before it had reached five hundred feet, the Gulfstream began turning to port, allowing Melissa to see the ground below more clearly. Another couple of bumps and the plane righted itself, then kept climbing.

Four hundred feet later, the plane made another turn to port, giving Melissa a different view of the ground below. Something caught her eye—a flash. Not much of one, only faint but enough of a presence to attract her attention. Then she frowned. A thin line seemed to appear in the air like someone had drawn it with a gray crayon. The line grew longer, then it started to curve as it tracked the plane.

Horror flowed through Melissa as she realized what it was. As she opened her mouth to shout a warning, she knew it was too late.

The FIM-92 Stinger slammed into the Gulfstream at seven hundred and fifty meters per second. The resulting explosion blew the aircraft in two, killing everyone on board.

CHAPTER 20

Worldwide Drug Initiative, El Paso, Texas

There was a soft knock, and the door swung open to reveal Ferrero standing in the hallway. He entered the office, closing the door behind himself. Thurston asked, "Are Reaper and his team on the ground?"

"Just touched down. They're moving toward their target as we speak."

"Good."

She noticed the troubled expression on his face. "What is it?"

"A CIA-chartered plane crashed not long after takeoff in Washington an hour ago. Melissa Smith was on board."

A cold hand gripped Thurston's heart and squeezed it until she felt like she couldn't breathe. "Are...are you sure?"

"Yes."

"How? What happened?"

"No one knows yet. Too early to tell, but one eyewitness reported that it exploded in midair."

"It was them. It had to be," she snarled.

"We don't know that."

"Who else could it be?"

He knew she was right. He'd had the same feeling when the news came through. "If they knew she was coming, they had to find out somehow."

Thurston nodded. "Pull Slick from whatever he's doing and have Teller take over. I want my office swept for everything."

"I'll take care of it. But if they knew about Melissa, they know everything or almost everything. No one is safe."

"Fuck it," she hissed. "Tell Reaper if that bitch is there, I want her more than ever. I'll waterboard her until she gives me everything she knows about the fucking Cabal."

———

Washington, DC

Hank Jones was on his way home when it happened. His driver was traveling on Sixteenth Street past Rock Creek Park when suddenly he turned off into Morrow Drive, going from bright streetlights to almost complete darkness.

"Ernie, what are you doing?" Jones asked the driver.

Ernie said nothing.

"Come on, Ernie, I asked you a question."

The SUV bounced over a bump and kept going. A couple of turns later, they were on Ross Drive. "Damn it, Ernie, what the fuck is going on?" Jones demanded.

Ernie pulled off to the side and came to a sudden stop. Lights came on in front of them from a second vehicle. Ernie almost sobbed as he said, "I'm sorry, General, I-I didn't have a choice. My family—"

Jones suddenly realized what was happening. He felt a wave of calm sweep over his body as he accepted his fate. "It's all right, Ernie. It's all right."

The general reached for the door handle and opened the door. If he was going to die, he wasn't going to take it sitting down. He'd stand up and face it head-on. He slid out of the back seat and stood beside the vehicle.

Four men alighted from the vehicle in front. One of them said, "Walk forward."

Jones did as he was directed.

One of the men went past him to the driver's side window and coldly shot Ernie in the head through the glass.

"What the fuck did you go and do that for, you bunch of gutless pussies?"

"It's just the job," the man who'd spoken earlier said.

"Fuck you and your job. Who ordered this? Huh? Going to tell me? Getting too close, are we?"

The man raised his weapon to fire, and Jones thrust out his chin in one last act of defiance. The air was suddenly filled with angry lead hornets. The four killers jerked violently and fell to the ground, unmoving.

Out of the darkness and into the headlights emerged three shooters dressed in jeans and t-shirts. All had on tactical vests and ballistic helmets with NVGs attached. They ignored Jones briefly as they checked the fallen killers. Then their leader turned to the general and said, "Sorry we're late, sir."

Jones grunted. "I'd say you were just in time, Chief."

"Let's get you out of here, sir," SEAL Chief Borden Hunt said.

Jones looked back at his vehicle and to the driver slumped in the front seat. Hunt put a hand on his shoulder. "He's gone, sir. We need to leave now."

Jones nodded. "Lead the way, Chief."

Hunt turned to his men. "Popeye, Rucker, move out."

All four of them disappeared into the dark.

Worldwide Drug Initiative, El Paso, Texas

"You were right, Mary, they went after Hank Jones," Ferrero told her.

She stopped what she was doing and held her breath before releasing it. "Is he—"

"He's fine. Scimitar and his boys got there just

in time."

"Thank God for that."

Ferrero nodded. "There's something else."

Thurston sighed. "There always seems to be lately. Hit me with it."

"Two more bodies just popped up in the DC area. One was a senator from Wisconsin, and the other was an ex-Marine general."

"Murder?"

"Preliminary findings on one is a heart attack, and the other is a stroke. Both were names on the list."

"Ares is cleaning house. We can expect more, I think."

"Maybe. How do you want to proceed with the rest of the names we have?"

"We're going to have to sit on them. We can't prove anything. They are only names on a piece of virtual paper."

"Do you wish to proceed with the Montana mission?"

"Hell, yes. If we get that bitch, we might just have something."

"Slick showed me the picture."

Thurston stared at him.

"How the hell do we deal with this going forward?"

"I don't know."

"You know we can't touch him, even if we get Rosalie Spalding. Melissa Smith was a warning to tell us he can get to us anytime he wants."

Thurston nodded. "And that's the worst part.

What do you propose?"

"We do like the general said. Take her off the board."

"What about Ares?"

"We'll get him. Eventually."

Thurston contemplated what Ferrero had just said. "All right, tell Reaper about the change of orders. We'll get target confirmation and drop a Hellfire on her. Agreed?"

"Yes, ma'am."

Bright Spark Solutions Base ***1, Montana

"Change of plan," Kane whispered to Cara. "We've been ordered to confirm the presence of the target and then let Bravo One take over."

"They're going to frag her ass?"

"Yes. Once that's done, we're out."

"What the hell is going on, Reaper? What aren't we being told?"

"I don't know."

"Bravo? Reaper Two, copy?" Cara said into her comms.

"Copy, Reaper Two."

"Ma'am, don't take this the wrong way, but how about you tell us what the fuck is going on? You're holding something back, and we deserve to know what it is."

"Shit," Kane hissed beside her.

There was a drawn-out silence before Thurston said, "All right. Yes, you do. We think we know who Ares is."

The general went on to tell her what they knew and finished by saying, "And at this point in time, we can't do shit about it."

"Thank you for your honesty, ma'am. Reaper Two, out."

Cara looked at Kane and said, "We need to get that bitch out of there."

Kane shook his head. "No. We stay with our orders."

"Damn it, Reaper! How the hell do we fix this if we don't have her?"

"We have the list. We work that. We follow the money."

Cara snorted. "And in the meantime, Ares keeps on keeping on without any checks."

"We'll get him," Kane told her. "Now we just wait for the sun to come up and confirm our target."

"All right, we'll do it their way."

———

Cara swept the interior compound once more, looking for target confirmation. The scope on her CSASS gave her the view she needed for a positive ID. It was around ten in the morning, and the sun was now high in the sky over the pine-clad mountains that surrounded the base.

There was movement beside her as Kane and Axe crouched. "How's it going?"

"If this keeps up, I'll be walking around with one eye like a damned pirate," she growled.

Axe said, "Give me your weapon and take a rest."

Cara passed it over, and the big man settled in behind the scope. Cara rolled onto her back and asked, "Anything more from home?"

"Nothing."

"The bird?"

"On station. Has been for a while now."

"Hey, guys, we've got movement. Looks like our target is on site."

"Typical." Cara grunted. "I do it for hours, then I hand it to the gorilla and bingo."

Axe looked at her. "What can I say? I'm lucky with the ladies."

"Call it in."

"Bravo One, this is Reaper Four, copy?"

"Copy, Reaper Four."

"I have eyes on target. Coordinates—"

Axe rattled off the numbers and waited for confirmation.

"Reaper Four, we have good confirmation of the target. We're ready to fire."

"Frag the bitch."

EPILOGUE

Worldwide Drug Initiative, El Paso, Texas

"While reports are still coming in about yesterday's explosion at the Bright Spark training base in Montana, all the press knows at this time is that there were a number of casualties, including six dead. The President—"

"What now?" Kane asked as he switched the monitor off. He turned to face the other three people in the room with him.

"Business as usual," General Hank Jones stated.

"How can you go back to that after what was done to you?"

Jones gave a grim smile. "I've got new bodyguards. Alex has let me have Scimitar and his boys. Besides, I don't think much will happen for a while. Ares knows we can't touch him without evidence, and us eliminating Rosalie Spalding saw to that."

"We still have the list," Kane pointed out.

"A list that means nothing without evidence."

"We have account numbers, so we can get at the money."

"Empty. Every last one of them."

"Shit."

"Their time will come, Reaper, but not just yet. We have to wait."

"Until when, General?" Kane demanded. "Given what we know, we're all targets for them."

"Maybe. But they've taken hits over the last few days, so they'll be reorganizing. The war in Colombia has been called off, and negotiations are to begin within the next week or so to address the drug problem."

"What about the trizanthium?"

Jones smiled. "Somehow, word of that leaked, and it is being included as part of the bargaining that is sure to take place."

"But Harris could still get the rights to mine it," Thurston pointed out.

"He could, but so could any number of mining companies who apply. It will be all down to the Colombian government."

Ferrero sighed. "So, we wait."

"Yes, we wait."

———————

Somewhere in Washington, DC

Ares sat in the room with four other persons—his new lieutenants, who for the first time he had allowed to see his face. On the walls around him were six monitors. Each had a caption at the bottom: Great Britain, France, Belgium, Australia, Italy, and Germany. To go with them were names like Aphrodite, Artemis, Apollo, Athena, Adonis, and Hades. Each figure was blacked out. Like Ares, they were the leaders of the Cabal in their regions. And like Ares, they had cleansed their ranks of those who had failed them. Now they faced a bigger threat. They had been forced out of the shadows into the light, and that would need rectifying.

"What do you propose to do, Ares, about the new threat we face?" Athena asked.

"We must regroup and fall back into the shadows where we live to plan once more."

"We were all counting on the trizanthium, Ares," Artemis said gruffly. "Now we have nothing."

"There is still a possibility of securing it," Ares reminded them.

"You have been careless, Ares," Apollo scolded him. "If we are to succeed in our vision, you need to do better."

Ares bristled. Who the fuck did Apollo think he was? "Watch your tongue. None of you would be where you are today if it weren't for me."

"This is not about the individual, Ares. It's about the collective."

"You are right. I apologize." The sarcasm in his voice was obvious.

"How long must we wait?" Hades asked.

"It will be a little longer than we first thought," Ares allowed.

"And what about the Russians? They get stronger while we wait."

"Nothing has changed as far as they are concerned."

"What about those responsible for the trouble we faced?"

"They are no longer a threat," Ares explained.

"Did you kill them?" Athena asked.

"No, but I sent them a warning."

"A warning? What good is a warning? They must be dealt with."

Ares nodded. "You are right. I will see to it."

"Do it quietly, Ares," Adonis snapped. "We cannot afford any more distractions. It takes focus away from the big picture and everything we're trying to achieve."

The screens went blank, and Ares turned to those seated in the room with him. "You heard what the Cabal ordered. See that it's done. Do not fail."

A LOOK AT: DEADLY WATER BY BRENT TOWNS AND SAM TOWNS

FROM THE AUTHOR OF THE ACTION-PACKED TEAM REAPER SERIES COMES A NEW PAGE-TURNER YOU WON'T WANT TO PUT DOWN!

A car bomb in a quiet suburban street sets in motion an investigation which will uncover the tentacles of organized crime stretching from the water-starved outback to the halls of power in the country's capital.

Senator Colin Worth was about to introduce a water bill which would cost the big producers millions before he was assassinated. However, the trail—as investigated by Detective Sergeant Gloria Browning and her team—only throws up more questions than answers.

Meanwhile, former undercover operative Dave Nash is brought in to investigate the disappearance of a water inspector in the town of Collari, on the Barwon River. But things take an even darker turn when Gloria's daughter, Rachel, is abducted.

Now, to get her back, Nash has to go against an organization who feeds its victims to the trees.

AVAILABLE NOW

ABOUT THE AUTHOR

A relative newcomer to the world of writing, Brent Towns self-published his first book, a western, in 2015. Last Stand in Sanctuary took him two years to write. His first hardcover book, a Black Horse Western, was published the following year. Since then, he has written a further 26 western stories, including some in collaboration with British western author, Ben Bridges.

Also, he has written the novelization to the upcoming 2019 movie from One-Eyed Horse Productions, titled, Bill Tilghman and the Outlaws. Not bad for an Australian author, he thinks.

He says, "The obvious next step for me was to venture into the world of men's action/adventure/thriller stories. Thus, Team Reaper was born."

A country town in Queensland, Australia, is where Brent lives with his wife and son.

For more information:
https://wolfpackpublishing.com/brent-towns/

Made in the USA
Las Vegas, NV
24 April 2021